I0451463

Tessa's Trio

An Erotic Ménage Novel

Katie O'Connor
Snarky Heart Press

Tessa's Trio

Katie O'Connor

ISBN: 978-0-9881281-2-5

Author may be contacted by email at
katieoconnorwrites@gmail.com.

Cover Design by: Jenn Howard

Dedication and Acknowledgments

This one is for the Spawn: my two darling daughters, Tina and Wendy. Girls, you bring so much joy and happiness into my life. You inspire me to do my best to make you proud. Thanks, girls.

Thanks to Jenn Howard for the fabulous cover. Thanks to Deb, Sandra, JoAnne, Brenda, Alyssa and Tamara for the editing. It fascinates me that every editor finds something different to tweak and correct. As always, any remaining mistakes are my own.

Chapter One

"You know that I'm only going under protest," Tessa reminded her long-time friend. "I hate bars. I hate parties, and frankly I'm not all that thrilled about men right now." She crossed her arms over her chest and glared. Becky's laughter surprised Tessa.

"You are such a liar." Becky shook her finger in Tessa's face. "You like going to bars and dancing. You love parties, and more than that, you love men. You're just pissed that Rick cheated on you and you had to dump him. He won't be there, I checked. He's gone to Mexico with that new skank of his." Turning back to the mirror Becky ran a brush through her short black hair, spritzed a bit of hairspray into it and straightened her large breasts inside her bra before declaring herself done. "Now, get over here and we'll have you ready in no time."

"I…don't…want…to…go," Tessa repeated.

"Yes…you…do. And you damn well know it. I can't figure out why you are protesting. Everyone will be there. We'll have a couple of beers, some conversation, some unwinding, all followed by a good night's sleep. It's the perfect way to end a stupidly long day." She crooked a finger at her friend who heaved a huge sigh and sat down at the dressing table. "We won't mess with your hair." She touched a corkscrew curl with a hint of reverence. "Every woman I know would kill for this hair."

Tessa smiled at her friend's generous compliment. It was true; her hair was her best feature. She studied herself in the mirror. Her hair fell to just past her shoulders in perfect corkscrew curls of golden brown, and in the sun, it shone with red highlights. She didn't know which ancestor has gifted her with her curls rather than her sister's poker-straight, fine hair, but she thanked them. She inherited the best hair; her sister got the generous, sexy breasts. Tessa looked down at her own B-cups and shrugged. While they weren't big, they were pretty, with perky pinky-brown nipples that loved being nibbled. Somewhere out there was a man who didn't care how big they were. It just hadn't been her no-good, cheating ex, Rick, despite his professions to the contrary.

"Come on Tessa, it will be fun. Paste on a smile and let's go." Becky made faces at Tessa in the mirror until she laughed.

Tessa's smile dropped away. "I'm not ready to date again," she warned her friend. "I get queasy just thinking about it. How could I not know that Rick was screwing around on me? I feel like such an idiot. I'm twenty-six, an adult. I should have seen the signs, we dated for three years. We were all but engaged and I didn't realize he had a tart on the side? His double-D secretary, after he claimed to prefer small breasts? Am I really that blind?" Disbelief colored her voice. She shook her head and sighed. It still hurt that he had cheated.

Becky rested her hands on Tessa's shoulders and massaged them lightly. "You knew; you just refused to see it. Remember Christmas? Come on; he was suddenly sick and couldn't spend the day with you."

"That was weird, because he was fine on Boxing Day," Tessa admitted, leaning into her friend's relaxing massage. "I thought he would be sick for days. He said he had a horrible case of food poisoning."

"And he didn't want you to come over and play nurse. And, how many dates did he cancel at the last minute?" Stroking softly, she urged Tessa to relax.

"Damn." Tessa slapped her hands onto her legs. "And the fucking trips out of town." Closing her eyes, she took four deep breaths. "I knew. I just didn't want to admit it. Why didn't you say something?" She glared at her friend.

"You were happy. Blind, but happy and I trust you. I knew that you would figure it out yourself, eventually." Patting Tessa's shoulders lightly, she added, "Buck up, let's go have a couple of beers and a few laughs. I promise not to try to hook you up." She grinned and winked.

"No fix ups? No pressure?" When Becky nodded, Tessa added, "Pinky swear." She held out her baby finger.

A barking laugh escaped Becky and she stuck out her baby finger. "Pinky swear? What are we, first graders?" They shook fingers and she dropped a kiss on Tessa's head. "You're as close to a sister as I've got and I just want to look after you, but I promise not to try to hook you up." She paused before adding, "At

9

least for tonight. You will get over him." Becky handed Tessa some lip gloss.

"God, I hope so." She dutifully applied the gloss, but refused to embellish herself any further except for a quick spritz of perfume. Looking into the mirror, she smiled at her friend. "I'm really not dressed to go out," she protested mildly, knowing she was wasting her breath. There was no way she would fit into Becky's clothes. Becky was four inches taller and very well endowed. At only five feet four and with her small breasts, there was no way they could share clothing. Her knee length denim skirt and white linen sleeveless top would just have to do.

For a moment she wished she had worn heels, and then decided she was glad she hadn't. They killed her feet and if she was going to be standing all night, her sparkly flat sandals were a much better choice. Since Becky's clothes were out of the question and home was a forty-five-minute round trip, she would have to do. "Let's go. I have to socialize eventually."

It only took them a few minutes to arrive at the local watering hole with the uninspired name of "The Pub". The place was packed. Standing room only. Working their way slowly around the other patrons, Becky and Tessa wormed their way to the far corner where their friends had gathered. As they twisted and wiggled through the crowd, Tessa was certain that some of the bumps and touches she felt were deliberate. One woman looked her right in the eye as her hand slid across Tessa's groin. As her hand wandered, she smiled broadly and winked, sending a rush embarrassment through Tessa. Women had never moved her, and it made her uncomfortable when one expressed interest. Too bad her friend Shayla wasn't here. The bold woman and Shayla might have hit it off. She seemed Shayla's type.

Reaching their group, Tessa worked her way around to chat with a couple of friends leaning against the back wall. The music was loud, the pub-chatter louder, and the room was filled with sounds of laughter. A person had to shout to be heard, and on occasion when the general hubbub dimmed, an outrageous comment could be heard loud and clear. A party atmosphere prevailed. It smelled like alcohol, chicken wings, and cologne. It sounded like tonight's lacrosse game had come out the right way for this crowd.

Tessa sipped at the beer Becky handed her and melted into the conversations around her. Becky had been right, she did love this. It appealed to the voyeur in her. She loved to take it all in, snooping and eavesdropping on the conversations going on around her. People fascinated her; she loved watching and listening to them.

She enjoyed meeting new people and getting to know them, but she was more comfortable one-on-one, or in a small group, than she was in a crowd. Tonight, surrounded by her friends, she laughed and joked, taking as much teasing as she was giving.

A petite blonde eased her way into the group. "Tessa, how are you holding up?"

Tessa hugged her friend, smiling wryly. "I'm okay, Mia. Getting better."

They fist bumped. "Excellent. You'll be fine. Give yourself some time. Let your heart heal, but don't blind yourself to the opportunity to love. Opportunity only knocks once." Mia laughed. "And you don't want to miss Mr. Right."

"You are such an incurable romantic."

"True, but I don't want a cure. Mr. Right-for-me is out there somewhere. And he's out there for you too. Never give up, Tessa. Never give up." Her eternal optimism lit her face.

The rest of Mia's words were lost to Tessa. Across the room, a tall, dark haired man caught Tessa's eye, distracting her. He had the sexiest smile she had seen in ages. Whoa, who was he? She craned her neck for a better look. Holy hell, he was gorgeous and he was talking to someone she knew. While they weren't friends, Tessa had known Kim since high school. Should she go over and talk to Kim and get an introduction?

The decision was taken away from her when he looked directly at Tessa with a broad smile. She couldn't help but smile in response. He tipped his head in acknowledgement and turned back to his conversation. She decided that it would be a waste if she didn't get to see that hot smile close up. Counting on Kim to introduce them, Tessa set her virtually untouched beer on the table, excused herself from her friends, and shimmied her way through the crowd toward that enticing smile.

"Kim, how are you?" Tessa stopped beside Kim. "I haven't seen you in months."

Kim pulled her into a fake, girlie hug, air kissed both of Tessa's cheeks and gushed, "Oh my god, Tessa. It's been so long." Kim's attitude was why Tessa didn't spend much time around her; the woman dripped insincerity. If there was one ounce of genuine feeling in her it was well hidden behind a thick wall of forced, gushing enthusiasm.

"How is Rick?" Kim asked slyly.

"Oh, I don't know." Tessa said breezily. "We're not together anymore." Tessa pasted a false smile on her face. Fucking bitch, she thought, she knew damned well he cheated on me. The two-timing bastard is lucky she didn't cut his nuts off. "How is …" She paused meaningfully. "Mark? It was Mark you were seeing the last time we talked; wasn't it?" She managed to make her voice sound innocent and enthusiastic.

"It was Tim," Kim snipped. "We aren't dating. We're just friends." Her voice held a hint of anger.

Direct hit, Tessa thought, knowing she would regret her catty behavior later. Tessa smiled. "Sorry. My mistake. I thought you guys were…kind of an item." They glared at each other. Kim had always had the ability to anger Tessa. They had started arguing the first time they met in high school and hadn't stopped since. Sometimes, it was in good fun, but often it had a mean, designed-to-hurt undertone. It confused Tessa and often she wondered why they rubbed each other the wrong way.

Mr. Sexy Smile shifted uncomfortably during the exchange, his gaze pivoting between them as they fired shots back and forth. There was a history here; that much was obvious. He looked from one woman to another. They were both pretty, but the newcomer had something about her that caught his attention, even from across the room. These bickering girls made him want to bury his hands in her hair and pull her close for a kiss. He had noticed her the moment she entered the bar and had tried extracting himself from Kim, hoping to make his way towards the woman Kim had called Tessa.

13

He rolled the name around in his mind. Nice. It suited her somehow. Pretty, but not extravagant. She didn't need the embellishment of a fancy name. He found himself wanting to touch her cheek to see if it was as soft it looked.

It dawned on Tessa that Kim thought she was poaching on her territory and wouldn't be offering an introduction. She didn't want to pass up the opportunity to meet him, to talk to him. So, mustering up her courage, Tessa turned to him and smiled.

"Hi." She offered her hand. "I'm Tessa Dupree. You must be Kim's friend." It was all she could do to spit the words out. Her throat was dry and she was uncharacteristically nervous. Usually she didn't hesitate to talk to a stranger, so why did she feel so…so disconcerted?

"It's nice to meet you, Tessa. I'm Peter White." He smiled, and offered his hand. Tessa was pretty sure she heard Kim growl so she flashed a quick, conciliatory smile and turned her attention back to Peter.

"Nice to meet you Peter." Their hands met, his huge calloused one engulfing her small hand and squeezing gently. He cupped her hand between his. His touch was soft and felt very intimate and personal as his thumb caressed hers. Shivers raced up her arm and her breath caught in her throat.

Tessa looked up into his eyes. Geez, he was tall and he had the most beautiful brown eyes she had ever seen. He smiled at her, revealing a sexy dimple. His short dark hair was well trimmed giving him a proper, professional air that was completely at odds with his cheeky grin. He placed her hand in the crook of his elbow. His eyes sparkled. He said, "Can I buy you a drink?"

Katie O'Connor

Chapter Two

What was he saying? Tessa's mind raced. She was completely and totally distracted by his touch and his words rattled around her brain unheard. She was speechless from the tingles of electricity running through her. It took a moment for her mind to get around the sensations wracking her body.

What was had he said?

Oh yeah, a drink. He wanted to buy her a drink. Tessa nodded her agreement and they edged through the crowd toward the bar. Tessa spared Kim a quick glance over her shoulder. Kim glared at Tessa, who waggled her fingers in a mock wave. Wow, if looks could kill!

Once they were away from Kim, Tessa was startled to hear Peter say, "I'm glad you showed up. I was looking for a way to politely extract myself. Your friend is a little aggressive for my tastes."

"She can be a bit forward," Tessa agreed, hoping he didn't think her too bold for introducing herself, but quickly discarded the thought because he had acknowledged her earlier.

He grimaced and shrugged. "Sorry, that was inconsiderate of me. Mom always told me to keep my mouth shut if I didn't have anything nice to say. But my friends have all vanished for the night; and I was heading out when she latched on me and I've been trying to break away ever since." He smiled down at Tessa. "Then I saw you come in with your girlfriend and was hoping for a chance to meet you, and maybe talk to you."

"Oh." She blushed. "Here I am, talk away." It wasn't difficult to talk to Peter. He was engaging, attentive and seemed to know when to fill the blank spots in their conversation, and when it was simply a natural pause.

They stood side by side at the bar, their shoulders almost touching. Tessa flagged down the bartender, who had been a high school friend, and after a moment of catching up with Tessa, he brought them each an icy draft beer.

"So," she asked Peter, "What brings you to The Pub tonight?"

"I was at the game with some friends and we stopped in for a drink." He smiled at her. "I didn't notice you at the game." His tone implied that he would have seen her if she had been there.

The idea that he might have noticed her in the large crowd was thrilling. "No, we couldn't make it. We worked late today. Becky and I just thought we would join the celebration." His fingers brushed hers and she clenched her hand into a fist to keep from caressing him back. Forcing her hand to relax, she wondered where the sudden rush of need had come from. He had the strangest effect on her.

That first touch of his hand seemed accidental, but she quickly realized that Peter was a master of the casual touch, his fingers brushing hers and moving away. His thigh bumped into her leg, pressed and backed off. His foot rubbed against hers for the merest fraction of a second. His shoulder grazed hers as he shifted his stance. Each bump and brush made her heart pound and her pulse race. Once she thought she felt his hand brush across her ass, but the sensation was so light and fleeting that she wondered if she had imagined it. When he reached up and slipped a wayward curl back behind her ear Tessa went moist with desire and her knees grew weak. Fortunately, a table opened up nearby and they were able to sit down before she fell down or dragged him outside where they could be alone.

They settled into the secluded table by the wall and sat looking at each other. "So, tell me about you. What makes Tessa tick?" He stroked her hand lightly before cupping it in his. "What do you do for a living?"

Staring into his eyes, it was a moment before his words registered. "Ah, I'm a unit clerk at the hospital. I help with the charting and all the paperwork."

"I'm sure there's more to it than just paperwork," he cajoled.

"Absolutely, but I don't want to bore you with my job. What about you? What do you do?"

"Office stuff." He shrugged. "What's the best part of your job?"

"No way," Tessa declared. "You're not getting off that easily. What do you do?" She pinned him with a stare, and tried to ignore the soft stroking motion of his thumb on the back of her hand.

"I'm a district manager for a petroleum company." He took a long slow sip of his beer without taking his gaze off of Tessa.

Wow. She wanted to be that beer. Tessa almost laughed at the crazy thought, until his tongue darted out to lick a stray drop of glistening liquid off his lip. Oh yeah, she definitely wanted to feel his mouth and tongue on her. She shifted restlessly in her seat, trying to ignore the heat pooling low in her belly.

"You have beautiful eyes," he told her with a smile. "I adore the way they look like creamy caramel, and how they sparkle when you smile. They're lovely."

She flushed a little and tried to turn the conversation back to him. "How was the game tonight?"

"It was good. The team I was cheering for won. But it would have been better if I had been watching it with you." He raised her hand to his mouth and kissed her softly on the knuckles.

His lips brushed like a whisper over her skin and when he turned her hand over to caress her lightly on the palm, she thought she would melt.

"Oh," she whispered, almost soundlessly, and grabbed frantically at her glass for a drink to moisten her suddenly dry throat. She stared at Peter, entranced, and wondered what part of her he would touch next. Breathlessly, she waited to see where he would lead her.

"Heya, Tessa." Becky's voice jarred Tessa back to reality.

"Becky." Tessa jerked her hand from Peter's grasp and stared at her friend.

"I'm headed home. Are you coming with me?" Becky smiled smugly at her friend, clearly enjoying the fact that she had interrupted an intimate moment.

"Um." She looked at Peter, who raised one eyebrow at her, almost daring her to stay. "No, I think I'll hang out for a bit. Unless you need a ride." She fumbled the words as Peter took her hand back in his and resumed stroking her skin.

"I'm good; Mia said she would drive me. Who's your friend?" She smiled warmly at Peter.

Tessa bristled. "Becky Markham, meet Peter White."

"Nice to meet you Peter." Becky offered her hand and a warm smile.

Peter shook her hand perfunctorily and said, "Nice to meet you too," before releasing her hand and turning his attention back to Tessa.

Happiness soared through Tessa. It wouldn't have been the first time Becky had unintentionally stolen a man from Tessa. It was all she could do not to crow in triumph when Peter virtually ignored her friend.

"Well, later then," Becky said. "Catch you at work tomorrow. Text me later if you need anything. I'll have my phone handy all night." She gave Peter a look of warning which he ignored. Shaking her head, she walked away from the pair.

Tessa gave a half-hearted wave and said good night, but her attention had turned to Peter and the rhythmic touch of his fingers on the inside of her wrist. She took a large sip of her beer, trying to still the jitters of anticipation coursing through her. She had only just met him, but her body was crying out for his, demanding more than simple hand holding.

Half way through her beer she realized that she was light-headed, her body on fire and almost quivering with need. She wasn't drunk, not even close, but she was aroused almost beyond belief. What was it about Peter that intrigued her so much? Was it his gentlemanly manners, his soft touches, the fact that he paid attention to her ideas and opinions? Was it the sparkle in his eyes, his sexy smile or that super-hot dimple?

She tilted her head and studied him, idly twirling a curl around her fingertip. He wasn't handsome, exactly. He was cute. His dark brown hair was neatly trimmed, his t-shirt was neat, his shorts pressed. All in all, he was simply sex on a stick and Tessa was finding him almost irresistible.

When his foot brushed hers under the table she pulled back for an instant and then thought, to hell with it, and slipped her own sandal off. Trailing a toe across the top of his foot, she explored his foot thoroughly before sliding her toes up the inside of his calf and back down again.

Peter trailed his toe up the outside of Tessa's other leg, lingering at the knee before curving his foot around her leg and stroking her calf on his way back down. Lightning tingles raced through her, her legs quivering, her groin growing damp. They played the back and forth game for a while, trying to remain focused on a semi-intelligent conversation, but for Tessa, talk was becoming increasingly difficult.

She squirmed in her chair, slipped off her other shoe and trailed both feet up his legs and nestled them in his lap. His eyes widened in shock and he drew a startled breath before relaxing and continuing their discussion. His cock hardened and twitched under her wiggling toes.

He touched her hand as they talked. His fingers traced hers, his touch light and teasing, the contact hardly more than a whisper. Tessa's nipples peaked and she shifted restlessly, her feet pressing against the lovely bulge she could feel forming under his dressy shorts.

Peter leaned back and with soft hands eased her left foot off his lap. She hardly had time to form the thought that he might be rejecting her when she felt his foot slipping up the inside of her thigh, coasting higher, dipping under her short skirt until he pressed his toes firmly against the warm moist heat of her core. She pressed back against his foot, applying just the right amount of pressure to tantalize herself and make her want more.

"Would you like to dance?" he asked with a teasing smile, his toes wiggling against her heat.

Tessa tried to speak, but her suddenly dry mouth wouldn't form the words. She swallowed hard and tried again. "No thanks," she squeaked. Her legs were way too unsteady to hold her up for dancing, and dancing definitely wasn't what she had in mind. Who wants to dance, she thought, unless it's the Horizontal Mamba?

Their attraction was racing out of control; for Tessa it was moving way too fast. She wondered why she had never felt this sudden, irresistible urge to sleep with a man before, but more than that, she wondered why she felt it now. "It's getting late and I have the early shift tomorrow." She couldn't resist rubbing his cock with the ball of her foot one last time. "I really should be going." She eased her foot down his leg and slipped back into her shoes.

She needed time to regroup and figure out where she wanted this flirtation to go. The only other time she had felt anything even close to this had been for her despicable ex. In the back of her mind she couldn't help but wonder if that should be a warning to her. Maybe she should leave and forget this crazy attraction had ever happened.

"Thanks for the drink." She rose to her feet, stumbling only a little on weak knees. "I really enjoyed myself." She was panicking, and knew it. Retreat seemed the best option.

"I'll walk you to your car," he offered. When she gave him a questioning look, he raised his hands in a gesture of mock innocence. "Nothing more," he promised. "I'll just make sure you get into your car safe and sound. A girl can't be too careful."

She tilted her head and gave him a quizzical look. When his expression remained innocent she gave a single nod and headed for the door. The crowd had thinned considerably and the pub was nearly empty. When had that happened? She had been so wrapped up in him that she had lost track of time and of her surroundings. She waved goodnight to Aaron, the bartender. When they stepped outside she was glad he had offered to escort her.

"Wow," she exclaimed looking around the nearly deserted lot. "This place is empty." She gestured to the far corner of the lot and headed that way. "My car is over here."

They walked towards the car, side by side, not touching at all. She stumbled a bit on an unseen rock and his hand shot out to steady her. When she had regained her balance, he slipped his arm around her waist, resting his hand against her hip and pulled her tight against his side.

The cool night breeze drifted across her skin, carrying a touch of his scent. Oh, he smelled so good. There was a hint of masculine cologne and something she couldn't quite identify. Pheromones, a distant part of her mind provided the word. Could a person actually smell pheromones? Her knees went weak again and she stumbled against him a bit. How could something as simple as his scent make her feel so, so weak and needy?

"Are you okay to drive?" he asked as they reached her car. "Should I call you a taxi?"

Tessa leaned against the car door and he leaned beside her. "I'm fine. I didn't even finish one beer. In …" she glanced at her watch, "three hours. Holy cow! I didn't realize we were talking that long." She tipped her head sideways to look up at him and smiled. Damned if she didn't love the way he towered over her. He had to be almost a foot taller than she was. She felt small and feminine beside him as she leaned against his side. Her hand snaked around his waist.

She took a deep breath, then another and felt tension shiver through her. It had been a very long time since she had been this aroused and all they were doing was standing side by side against her car.

"Time flies in pleasant company." He slid his arm around her shoulders, and his fingers pulled gently on one of her corkscrew curls, the slight tugging making her scalp twitch and her body feel…squirmy.

"Thanks," she whispered, somehow touched by the easy compliment. She dug in her pocket and found her keys, extracted them and rattled them gently. "Well, I should go." She leaned her head against his shoulder, knowing she had to leave, but loath to move from the cozy warmth of his side.

"Yes, you should," he agreed, his chin nuzzling her hair, his hand drawing idle circles on her arm.

She turned toward him a little more, nestling her head in the curve of his shoulder. She looked up at him. He was so handsome in the shifting shadows of the parking lot. She wanted to kiss him; she bit her bottom lip gently, and pushed out a soft sigh wishing she had the courage. She wanted, needed, to feel his lips against hers, to taste him and touch him. Her hands itched to stroke his chest and delve under his shirt to trace the plains of his abdomen and to find the peaks of his nipples. She breathed deeply, inhaling his scent, committing it to memory, saving it to savour later.

The night was cool, but she wasn't chilled. She was warm in the soft cocoon of his arm. "Okay," he whispered, "you have to go." He eased back a bit.

She looked up at him again and he smiled that sexy, very slightly crooked smile at her and she knew he was just as loath to separate as she was. There was something going on here, something between them. It was strong, electric, passionate, almost overpowering. She wiggled a bit and wondered if he knew how deeply he was arousing her just by standing beside her. Tipping her head further back, she looked at him, her mind screaming for him to kiss her. He moved forward, his head tilting just a fraction of an inch. He smiled at her again, his eyes flashing in the dark as he lowered his mouth and touched his lips softly to hers.

The contact was electric. Goose bumps rose on her arms, heat raced down her legs and moisture flooded her core. He could take her here, now, she was ready. She wouldn't need any coddling or preliminaries she was fully aroused, on the edge of orgasm just from that one soft touch of his lips to hers. Rising up on her toes she put her arms around his neck pulling him down toward her, deepening the contact, grinding their lips together. His tongue swept across her lips and she opened her mouth, granting him access, welcoming his moist invading tongue.

His kiss was soft, his lips firm. She pushed against him, pressing her body against his, revelling in his heat and tingling when she felt the evidence of his desire rising against her. Unbidden, Tessa's hips bumped forward and she felt him pushing back. His arms drew her closer, pulling her to him, deepening the kiss, taking, tasting, and demanding she respond.

She felt a light tugging as his hand tangled in her hair and felt a responding pulse, throbbing through her body. She clenched tight against a cock that wasn't there when his hands began roaming the curves of her body. He trailed his hand up and down her arm his touch light and teasing. His fingers drifted idly across her back and shoulders, exploring and caressing. Tessa stumbled against him, her knees weak. He tugged gently at her hair, making her moan and open her mouth wider for his questing tongue. He tasted of beer but she didn't mind. The hunger in her rose to meet him.

Peter's hand lingered at her waist, his fingertip marking slow, teasing circles. He paused a moment when her top lifted and his palm touched the heat of her naked back. Tessa's skin twitched and jumped at his tentative caress. Oh, don't stop! She breathed a sigh of relief when his hand moved higher, delving beneath her top, seeking more of her soft skin. Cool night air drifted under her shirt cooling her skin. He spread his hand and flattened it against her back, easing her even closer, his other hand fisting in her hair, controlling her head, angling her mouth where he wanted it. Tipping her head back, he teased his way along her chin line and nuzzled her ear, flicking gently with his tongue and trailing lower. Oh my, she thought, his lips feel so good.

A soft sigh escaped Tessa's throat as he kissed his way down the column of her neck and along her collarbone. Peter licked the hollow at the base of her throat before working his way up the other side to her ear with touches hardly more than a whisper. He nuzzled her ear, nipped it sharply with his teeth before moving on, back down her neck to tease her skin along the sweeping curve of her scoop-necked top.

Shivers raced through her and Tessa grasped his shoulders to keep upright, her knees weak and trembling. His tongue danced along her skin, marking soft damp circles along her neckline, teasing, tasting and pausing a moment to inhale deeply at the juncture of her breasts. Tessa sucked in her own startled breath at his soft groan of arousal. His mouth was pure heaven, but she wanted, needed more. Something about Peter called to her. This didn't feel like a random encounter, it felt like … more.

Her hands grasped at him, one moving to caress his head, to feel the softness of his hair, the other frantically exploring his chest and abdomen, then bravely dipping lower to caress him intimately. Briefly she had the thought that this wasn't like her. This level of urgent arousal was new and heady and she didn't care that they were standing in a parking lot, visible to any passers-by. The chance of being seen fuelled her ardour.

She cupped him gently, inhaling sharply at the feel of his hardness under her hand. Oh, he was so hard and long. He pulsed under her hand and his hips bucked against her. Peter pivoted slightly, trapping her against the car, one hand cupping her breast and the other pulling her left hand over her head and holding it there. She froze for a second, wary, but his hold was light, keeping in her in place but not threatening. The exquisite feel of his hand on her breast, his thumb stroking her nipple was too good to resist. She arched against him, moaning, encouraging him.

He pulled her neckline down and bent low to mouth her nipple through her bra. It pebbled under his touch as he sucked her through the lace. He teased and mouthed, his knee nudging its way between her legs then pressing upwards, gently, then more insistently until he was pressed firmly against her thin panties, her moisture hot against his thigh.

He pulled back and looked down at her; a soft, almost smug smile on his face. "You're dripping wet." He released her breast and trailed his hand lightly down her side, down her thigh to delve under her skirt. His fingers danced along her thigh, caressing as he edged toward her core. He stroked her through her panties, once, twice, and then slipped under them to caress her directly. He groaned aloud and devoured her mouth with a kiss as his fingers skated over her naked lips and he slipped one finger inside her.

Tessa writhed under his touch, her body on fire, her need building. She whimpered when he pulled his finger out and groaned when he raised it to his lips. Looking her right in the eye, he sucked it clean then delved in again for more. He teased and stroked, then slipped back inside and brought his fingers to her mouth. "Taste yourself," he demanded softly. "Taste how aroused you are." She turned her head away in denial. "Come on Tessa." He flicked his tongue across her ear. "Taste!"

Strangely powerless to resist his demand, she closed her eyes and turned back. Oh god, she wasn't really going to do this. Was she? Was she really going to taste her own pussy juice, just because he asked? She felt her mouth opening to accept his fingers.

"Look at me, Tessa. Look at me while you taste yourself." Again, she obeyed and opened her eyes. Peter's eyes flashed in the dark and as his finger slipped into her mouth and when she began sucking, she could almost swear she saw his eyes widen and pupils dilate.

Oh, this was so slutty, so hot. She was more aroused than she could ever remember feeling. Every sensation was intensified. Sight, sound, smell, touch, the sensations threatened to swamp her. The taste wasn't repulsive like she expected. His finger tasted salty and musky and she could smell the heat of her own arousal battling his light cologne and her own perfume. His body was scorching hot against hers, the car cool, but warming up where it pressed against her back.

His mouth returned to her breast, pushing her bra lower, exposing her to the night while his fingers delved back inside her, gently moving in and out until she began moving against him. Slowly, he increased the pace until she was writhing against him, her hips bucking, her mouth nuzzling his head, her hands roaming across his body, searching and exploring every bit that she could reach.

"Oh," Tessa breathed, knowing her orgasm was close. Too close. She was going to come against his thrusting fingers. She ground against him, but met nothing. He pulled his hand away.

"I have to taste you," he growled low and quiet. He nudged her sideways. "Up here." He patted the hood of the car and grasping her waist helping her hop up onto the front end of the car. "Lift," he demanded, tugging at her skirt, wiggling it higher, sliding her panties off and stuffing them into his pocket.

The hood was icy cold against her ass and she jerked upwards in shock. Peter pulled her into his arms, his legs nestled between hers and kissed her deeply, his hands foraging and exploring. Slowly he pressed her backwards until she was lying flat on the hood of the car, then he began his descent. He kissed her neck, her chest, and flicked the front clasp of her bra open and suckled her breasts, first one, and then the other.

"You are so lovely," he whispered. "You turn me on. I can't wait to taste you." He stroked and kissed her abdomen and moved to explore her thighs. He dropped his hands to caress her smooth lips. "Oh. So smooth and slippery. I love a smooth, wet pussy." He laid his hands between her legs and her belly, his thumbs caressing her moist heat. "Oh girl, you are so wet, so hot. I'm dying for you."

She wished he would stop talking; his words were so disconcerting, so arousing. She pushed against his thumbs, urging him on, begging without words for more. Her hips twisted and turned under his touch, aching, needing. Wanting. When his lips touched her she nearly bolted off the car. It felt so damned good. He kissed and licked her lips, teasing, tasting and when she thought she couldn't wait any longer, he darted out his tongue to touch her clit.

His hands pressed her against the car; his thumbs teased her lips, spreading them wide to allow access for his tongue. He flicked lightly across her clit, back and forth, up and down, seeking the perfect rhythm to drive her crazy. Her heart pounded, her breathing came in gasps and she bit her lips to keep from screaming. Desire pooled at the base of her belly, skittering electric jolts darted along her spine, tingled across her skin, and lodged in her pussy. She writhed, growing wet against his mouth. He sucked her clit into his mouth and flicked it with his tongue, and she exploded over the edge in a whirl of light and sensation. Her body twitching and shivering as he teased on and on, keeping her there, not letting her relax, fuelling her orgasm, making it last, until spent and complete, she pushed gently on his head, easing him away from her sensitive flesh.

To Tessa's surprise, she needed more. This was new. She had never, ever been multi-orgasmic, if that was the term. One had always been enough. But here, with Peter, she needed more. She needed him inside her. Pulling and clutching at his shoulders, she eased him upwards and straightened into a sitting position. He moved in and kissed her, smelling of her arousal and tasting like her pussy. The combination sent a jolt of lust flying through her and she fumbled with his belt.

Clumsy fingers impeded her progress and she growled, "Help me. I need you." Peter obliged by freeing himself quickly and easily, she took him in her hand, loving the long hard length of him and how he pulsed against her. When she moved to taste him, he backed off.

"Not this time, babe. I can't wait. I need you now." He took her mouth in a deep demanding kiss, grabbed her hips and eased her closer to the edge of the car. Fumbling in his pocket, he extracted a condom and before Tessa could draw two deep breaths he had it on. His hands found her breasts and as she arched toward him. She felt the tip of his cock nudging her opening and then driving home.

Tessa gasped as Peter slid in deep. She was stretched and filled like never before. His balls banged against her ass, his hair rubbed against her clit and she clenched around him.

"Geez," he groaned as she tightened against him. He slowly eased back, his motion so slow to be almost unfelt. Further and further back, until just the tip was in, then he pressed forward, sliding into her wetness as slowly as possible. For several long moments he teased her, easing in and out, kissing her deeply.

"Please," Tessa groaned. "More." Responding to her plea, Peter increased his pace, pumping in and out, slowly but steadily. "Harder," she begged her words mumbled into his lips. "Peter, please!" She writhed against him, bucking and wiggling matching his pace, trying to speed him up, her hands flying everywhere until they latched onto his ass. Digging her nails in deep she pulled him to her, slamming him in deep and hard. "Yes," she grunted.

Her desperation seemed to fuel his lust and he pumped harder, faster, driving in deep. She clenched around him, her pussy clutching and milking him. Her breaths came in choppy gasps, her words incomplete and incoherent as she begged for more.

She felt the first tingle start in her breasts, sending jagged twinges through her. Her nipples pebbled harder, her skin tingled and shivered, hot chills washed over her and her entire being focused on the heat throbbing of her groin. She bucked up, pressed herself against him, her hips moving in choppy jerks then stilling against him as she cried out her delight, spiralled higher and higher until she came apart in his arms.

Briefly aware of their location, Tessa muffled her cries of release by kissing him deeply. Her pussy clenched again and again against the rock-solid length of him. Deep inside, she could feel him pulsing against her moist core until he exploded inside her with a harsh cry of his own.

They stayed there, locked together for several long moments, recovering. Waiting for the world to stop spinning; waiting for their breathing to return to normal.

A car pulled into the lot, its headlights panning over them briefly. They exploded into action. Peter jerked away and helped her pull her skirt down and top up into place. To hell with refastening the bra! He fumbled with the fastening of his pants as the car came closer and then stopped. A door opened then closed. Footsteps sounded, coming toward them.

"Oh, God," Tessa murmured.

"You folks okay?" a deep masculine voice asked.

"Yes." Peter turned to look at the intruder. "Yes, officer."

Holy hell! We're...doing it on the car and a cop comes by. She wanted the earth to open up and swallow her whole.

"It's getting late," the officer warned, laughter in his voice. "Perhaps you folks should be headed home."

"Fuck off, Waters," Peter growled at the intruder who had the nerve to laugh.

"You know him?" Tessa asked. Geez, could it get any worse?

The footsteps came closer, a flashlight beam focusing in on the two of them, Peter standing in front of her protectively. "You all right, ma'am?" He asked, clearly enjoying himself.

"Um. Er. Yes." Her voice squeaked. She cleared her throat and tried again. "Yes officer. He was just helping me to my car." The officer laughed aloud at that.

"Get your ass out of here, White. It's time for you and your lady friend to head for home. It's late." He shone the light right in their faces. "Fix your clothes and get the hell out of here." The light went away, darkness returned and his footsteps retreated. After a moment the car door slammed and the engine started, but he didn't pull away.

"You know him?" Tessa asked again and groaned.

To her surprise, Peter just laughed. "He's my neighbour and best friend. And," he added, reluctance filling his voice, "he won't leave until you do." He leaned in and kissed her tenderly.

"You really need to go." He kissed her forehead and rested his head against hers. "Thank you for a lovely evening, Tessa. Can I have your number?" She nodded and he touched her cheek softly, gave her a hand down off the hood. She was in the car reaching for a pen when the cop tooted his horn at them.

"Shit, you better go. He'll just keep blowing his damned horn until you do." Peter leaned in to the car and helped Tessa with her seatbelt. They shared another quick kiss and he stepped back and closed the door.

Tessa rested her head on her hands and sighed before starting the car and taking off. She didn't even look back, she was too mortified. "Oh my god," she mumbled as she drove away. "What did I just do?" A thrill of excitement raced through her and she laughed, suddenly feeling light-hearted and happy.

Tonight wasn't the first time she had talked to a stranger in a bar, but she had never slept with a guy on the first date. What had she been thinking? And to fuck him in a parking lot, outrageous. She laughed again. Her friends would never believe this! As if she would tell them. It wasn't until she was almost home that she realized that they hadn't exchanged numbers, and for the life of her, she couldn't decide if that made things better or worse.

Peter stood for a moment watching Tessa leave. He smiled a soft smile. She was such a spitfire, and so different from the other women he knew. He had wanted women before, but not with such a frantic, burning need. And he had never, ever fucked in a parking lot before. He watched her tail lights disappear in the distance before he strolled cockily toward the cruiser. He climbed inside, looked at Waters and said, "Take me home Mitch. I'm in no shape to walk that far."

"What the hell were you doing?" Mitch asked him, putting the car into gear. "And in a parking lot too. Jesus man, you've got balls."

"She was hot, fucking hot and eager." He ran his fingers through his hair. "We talked for hours." He paused a second. "Son of a bitch! I didn't even get her number; because you kept honking the damned horn!" He punched the dash, making his friend laugh.

Chapter Three

Tessa and Becky hurried into Coffee and Cakes, a café-dessert specialty shop owned by their friend, Mia Platt. They were late, but that wasn't unusual for a work night. Things never went perfectly at the end of shift in a hospital. As a nurse, Becky had patients to see, and had to update the oncoming nurses as to the day's events. Tessa, a unit clerk, had an easier time of it, but for some reason the day was fraught with little issues and she had been running behind.

They slid into the booth with their friends, heaving out matching sighs of relief.

"Hey, chicks. We have arrived. Let tonight's meeting of the Gallery Girls commence." Becky greeted the four ladies already seated at the table.

Everyone groaned at the mention of The Gallery Girls. Years ago, when they were all in their early teens, they had met through a competition on a local radio station and had won photo shoots and modeling jobs at a local portrait studio. After a number of weeks working together on their shoots, some commercials and catalogue assignments, they had bonded as friends. In the years since, they had drifted apart and back together again a number of times. Now, their group friendship was as strong as ever. Recently, Kelly's father had passed on and she had inherited the portrait studio that had brought them all together.

"Sorry we're late," Tessa apologized with a grimace. "Today sucked, nothing went right."

Over the sympathetic murmurs from their friends, Becky stated, "That's just because you were exhausted from spending half the night with a strange man." Gasps and excited giggles exploded from the ladies.

"Oh, do tell!" Shayla demanded, her green eyes flashing with laughter. "This explains why you didn't answer your phone last night. Naughty girl." She wagged her finger in Tessa's face.

"There's nothing to tell," Tessa demurred. "I had a drink with a guy at The Pub last night. End of story." Her face flushed red. Please, please drop it, she pleaded silently. God, why did I even tell Becky about it? Tessa battled regret for her actions, for telling Becky, but most of all she battled the urge to grin and pump her fist in the air in triumph. Her lips curled up in a small grin.

Damned if last night hadn't been the most exciting night in her life. Her attraction to Peter had been electric and instantaneous. Plus, he could kiss like nobody she had ever met, and she wanted to kiss him again. And again. Well, she would like to see him again, if she had any idea how to find him.

"Oh, look at that grin," Megan gloated. "It's worthy of the Mona Lisa. No, worthy of the Cheshire Cat. You did have a good time, didn't you?" She gave Tessa a high five across the table. "About time."

"Did you finally purge the good-for-nothing Rick from your system?" Mia asked excitedly. "Tell us about your wild night."

"Okay, okay." Tessa caved. "Let me get a drink and I'll tell you all about it. Okay, maybe not all about it." Her friends groaned in unison. "Come on now, a lady does NOT kiss and tell."

Well at least not everything. There is no way in hell I'm telling you guys all the gory details, she thought.

While they waited for their orders, Tessa took a moment to study the women who had been her friends for years. They were a motley group from a variety of backgrounds, and now they were all successful career women who worked hard and played harder. Her friends had bodies of every shape and description; they had different quirks, abilities and irritations, but each and every one was near and dear to Tessa's heart.

She stifled a groan at the abuse she was going to take over her 'date' last night, but somehow, she couldn't wait to share the details. This was one for the record books. Of all the wild and crazy things she and her friends had done over the years, this one might just take the cake.

Settled in with their coffees and desserts, the group turned in unison toward Tessa, giving her expectant looks and urging her to spill her guts.

She raised her hands defensively and laughed. "Okay, okay. Last night after the game, Becky and I went to The Pub for drinks . . ." Tessa smirked as everyone leaned in close to hear the details. Obedient to the unwritten rules of The Gallery Girls, Tessa stretched the story out over several cups of coffee, giving all the details except the most intimate.

Her story ended with some kissing at the car, she kept the fact that the clothing started flying to herself. There was no way in hell she was going to tell them how far things had gone. They would not learn that Peter had stolen her favorite panties, or that they had been interrupted by a cop. She would never live either of those facts down.

"Anyone else date this week?" Tessa asked when then questions and begging for details had quieted down.

Becky raised her hand and grinned. "It wasn't this week, but I met this guy at work," she began.

"What?" Tessa cried. "You never told me you met someone. When was that?" Her voice cracked in her excitement. Becky hadn't dated for over a year after being burned by her ex.

"Last month," Becky clarified. "Remember that old guy in 316, the one with the dozens of kids and grandkids?" Tessa nodded. "His oldest son was in and had a bunch of questions. Usually he was decent, but that day he was rude, snappy and downright mean. But I'll be damned if he wasn't the sweetest hunk of man I've ever seen." She sighed and smiled. "He was getting louder and louder, and it was well after midnight and he should have been long gone. So, I took him to the chapel for a talk. It was the only quiet place I could think of."

"Point?" Blonde-haired, blue-eyed Kelly asked.

"My point is that he was about the best damned kisser I've ever met."

"You kissed him? I thought you said he was being an ass?" Tessa gave Becky a puzzled look. "And where was I during all of this?"

"On your break." Becky laughed.

"Did you get his number?" Mia quipped.

"I got his number all right. Right there on the middle pew in the chapel."

The group's questions stuttered to a halt and they stared at her dumb-founded.

"You did it in a chapel?" Megan whispered. "Holy shit. You're gonna burn! Did you a least get his name?" She laughed when her shock receded.

"Um, well, that is, not really." She sounded embarrassed. "I think it was Jim, Jock, or something like that. His last name was Young. Don't ask me how I remember that. Anyway, his dad went home before my next shift and I never got to talk to Jack-Jake-whatever again."

Tessa studied her friend and decided she seemed a little sad. She gave Becky a reassuring pat on the leg under the table. The look on her long-time friend's face told Tessa that Becky regretted not remembering the man's name. Becky was a fun-loving girl, but monogamy might as well be her middle name. A quick fling or one-night stand just wasn't her style, the girl rarely dated and when she did, it was one guy at a time and only men vouched for by friends.

"Can't you just call the old guy and get the stud's number?" Kelly asked.

"Hell no!" Becky and Tessa cried in unison.

Tessa added, "It's against hospital policy and she would get fired if anyone ever found out. No man is worth that risk." Even as she said it, Tessa wondered if Becky believed that as strongly as she did.

Slowly, conversation turned from men to things more mundane, like work, shopping and books. It was nearly four in the morning when the group finally broke up and headed home. Mia had sent her staff home hours ago, leaving their small group in the café. In the parking lot they said their goodbyes, excited to meet again in a few weeks to celebrate Tessa's birthday.

Shayla and Tessa lived in the same building, so Tessa caught a ride with Shayla, enduring her questions about Peter for the entire drive. It was a relief to close the apartment door on her friend's incessant questions and fall into bed for a nap before she headed to the airport to pick up her childhood friend Rob. After a long tour of duty away from home, Rob was finally getting some much-needed downtime and Tessa was excited to reconnect with her friend.

Chapter Four

Tessa paced back and forth in the airport waiting area. People came, picked up their baggage and went, but still there was no sign of Rob's flight. All the airline and arrivals board had to say was that it had been delayed. She had checked the internet just before leaving home and at that point her friend's flight had been listed as on time. Somewhere in between leaving home and arriving at the airport, things had changed drastically. The flight was almost an hour late and the harsh florescent lights and constant rumble of the PA system were wreaking havoc with her overtired brain.

She sipped her coffee, hoping the caffeine would give her a reprieve from the headache induced by her lack of sleep. Thankfully she had not been drinking last night. On occasion, meetings of The Gallery Girls got out of hand. The previous evening had been a late one, but alcohol-free.

As it was, she had spent the night tossing and turning, reliving the evening with Peter and wondering what the hell she had been thinking. Sex in the parking lot with a stranger? Was she insane? Never mind the embarrassment that she didn't know how to contact him if she had the guts to call. He had her panties in his pocket. Tessa groaned aloud. What the hell had she been thinking? She leaned against a post, out of the way of traffic to await Rob's arrival and decide what she was going to do about Peter.

On one hand, she could easily chalk it up to a one-night stand, even though that wasn't her usual style. On the other hand, that night had been some of the best sex of her life. There had been a connection between them unlike any she had ever experienced. Her first look at him had knocked her for a loop and his touch had been electric, but what had really surprised her was their ability to talk to each other and all the opinions they had shared.

"Tessa?" She was so wrapped up in her musings she completely missed the announcement that Rob's flight had arrived and didn't hear him calling to her.

Rob stood in front of Tessa, his kit at his feet and watched the expressions flit across her face. Her brows pinched in worry, she breathed a small sigh, and smiled softly. For a moment, her expression was tender and longing. Something had changed in his childhood friend. There was something different about her. She seemed both more relaxed, and more tense. Had she finally broken up with that dork Rick she had been dating for so long? He knew a sharp moment of fear as she smiled that tender smile again. Dang-it-all, she hadn't found another man already had she?

He studied her carefully, up and down. She had lost a few pounds, but he still knew every curve of that luscious body. They had been best friends and neighbours all through high school and had continued their friendship in the years since then. But not once had he worked up the courage to tell her how he felt about her. He had been hoping that now that Rick was out of the picture and he was on leave for a couple of weeks that he might have the long-awaited opportunity to pursue her. Damn, but he loved her, and if she had found another guy and he had to wait longer, he would. Even as he had the thought, he knew deep inside that if she had found another, it was time to move on. He would have to sever all his ties with her just to preserve his sanity.

Banking his feelings, he reached out and tugged gently on a curl of her hair. "Tessa," he spoke a little louder. "Where the heck are you, girl?"

She jerked back from the tug on her hair, her hands coming up defensively as she shifted into a kickboxing, defensive stance. "Back off creep," she teased when she realized who had interrupted her musings.

Rob laughed aloud. "Creep? Is that any way to treat your best friend?" He tugged her hair again, using the contact to draw her into his arms.

"Oh! Rob!" She relaxed her stance and slipped her arms around his neck. "I missed you." She pulled him up tight and kissed him soundly on the cheek. Resting her head on his shoulder she sighed. "I am so glad you're back." Eyes closed she breathed deeply, savouring his familiar masculine scent.

She sniffed once and sniffed again. Was that aftershave? She did a mental double-take. Why would he be wearing aftershave on his flight home from his deployment? It didn't make any sense. Had he met someone? Was he involved with one of the women in his unit? Her heart jumped and she swallowed a lump in her throat.

Oh my god. She wasn't interested in him romantically. Was I? What the hell? She stifled a mental sigh and tilted her head up to look at him to find him gazing down at her, a soft sexy smile on his lips, his deep blue eyes sparkling.

"Dang, you feel nice in my arms," he admitted. "I missed you."

Before she realized his intent, his head dipped and his lips brushed hers gently, then more firmly when she didn't pull away. A soft sigh escaped her and she realized that she wanted more. Rising up on her toes, she pressed her lips firmly against his and slid her arms around his neck. One hand stroked his soft, short blonde-hair; the other, gripped his neck pulling him closer. Rob groaned lowly against her lips and he deepened the kiss, his tongue darting out to taste her lips, his arms sliding around her waist. A heat raced through her, leaving her surprised and aroused.

She was attracted to him. My God, she's known him all her life and not once has she thought of him sexually. Had something changed in her? In him? Why was he suddenly so attractive, so damned hot?

Tessa pressed herself against him, revelling in the feeling of his firm muscular body against hers. He was only about five inches taller than she was, but Rob was firmly muscled, his body just the right side of bulky. Not lean, not weight-lifter heavy, he was firm and strong. His heat burned through her clothes, making her want to throw them off, to get closer. She wiggled a little, felt the rise of his arousal against her, and groaned low in her throat. Tessa felt Rob pull back slowly, his body easing back, creating space between them before ending their kiss.

"Wow," he murmured, his lips a scant inch from her own. "I think we'd better stop, for now, before we get arrested." He kissed Tessa lightly on the cheek and added, "You might be the most delicious thing I have ever tasted." He eased his hands from her waist and gripped her right hand in his left. He grabbed his kit with his free hand, and tugged her toward the door. "Come on, Kiddo, let's get out of here. I've got a hankering for some time alone with you."

"Okay," Tessa squeaked. Where was her voice? She cleared her throat. "How was the flight?" She squeezed his hand lightly and hastened her steps to walk alongside him.

"Good. Long. Boring. Let's talk about you." He winked down at her.

"Me? My life is boring." She snorted at her white lie. Her time with Peter had been anything but boring and ladies' night out last night had been a riot. But she was damned if she would share that encounter with Rob, even if he was her best friend.

Rob paused mid-step and looked down at her. "You snorted." He laughed. "Tessa Marie Dupree, you are lying to me." When she flushed he added, "Oh I'll bet there is a story here."

"Nope. No story. No sir. No way. No how," Tessa stammered in a rush, trying to evade his question. "I broke up with Rick." She didn't know why she added that, but suddenly it seemed important the Rob know that she was single.

"Well thank heaven for that," Rob declared, resuming walking toward the exit. "The guy was a dweeb and an asshole."

"Did you just say asshole?" Tessa asked in surprise. "You don't swear, ever."

"Well he was." Rob shrugged. "I don't know how you could stand to be around him. The rotten way he treated you used to just kill me. Which way to the car?" Rob asked, clearly uncomfortable with the conversation.

Tessa lead him to the car, popped the trunk and waited for him to stow his kit. Slamming the trunk, she looked him over, smiling softly. "Damn you look good in fatigues," she declared, stepping toward him and raising her lips to meet his. "Kiss me again," she whispered. "Let's see if it is as good this time as it was the first time."

Tessa smiled as Rob's eyes widened in surprise, even as he dipped his head to oblige her. His lips were firm, warm and soft. Her nipples puckered and her cleft moistened. Her arms slipped around his neck pulling him closer, dragging him near. She wanted to be close to him, to be part of him. Arousal swamped her and she moaned against his lips when his arms slid around her, his hands caressing her back. Tessa's tongue darted out to taste Rob but as the very tip touched his lips he pulled back.

"Tessa, we can't do this here." His hands stroked her back and hair soothingly. "We're in the middle of a parking lot for Pete's sake."

At the mention of Pete, Tessa went stiff and backed away. What was with her and parking lots lately? Dear god, was she going insane? Turning into some kind of exhibitionist? Holy hell! She shook her head to clear her errant thoughts and replied, "Yeah." Backing away on unsteady feet she wobbled her way to the driver's door and slid inside the car.

"Point me in the right direction," she told him. "I can't wait to see your new place. I still can't believe that I haven't seen it and you've been there for almost a year."

"What's so hard to believe? I'm on tour most of the time, and we spent my last home stretch camping, and you were in Kansas on that course for work when I moved in."

"I know, but it's been a year. You probably already know your neighbors and I haven't even seen your place. It's kind of sad."

"You should be used to that by now." He patted her knee gently. "You knew me long before I signed up. How many times in the past few years have we missed each other entirely when I was on leave?" She fell silent for a few moments. Her mind raced around a mental track, veering from arousal, to mortification, to lust, to chagrin, and back to arousal again.

Eventually, she knew she had to speak. "How long are you home for?" She spared him a quick glance as she navigated the busy freeway.

"I'm on leave for three weeks, but home for three full months. I have ninety-two days to enjoy your pretty face." He waggled an eyebrow at her. "Maybe I'll even get another one of those kisses. You're not dating anyone yet, are you?"

"Well, I met a guy I wouldn't mind getting to know better." She blushed deep red and avoided looking at him.

"One date?" Rob sounded incredulous. "Or more than one?"

"Well, one date. Sort of." Tessa sighed heavily. "It's hard to explain. I met him a couple of nights ago at The Pub." She shook her head and gave half an eye roll.

"Are you seeing him again?" Rob asked, his fingers tapping restlessly on his knee.

"No…" she trailed off, distracted by the Rob's heat as their bodies brushed together in her small car as she drove. Each touch of his shoulder and arm burned like a brand and sent her hormones skyrocketing.

"What about …," Rob gestured between them. "What about us?" he demanded. "That was some kiss you gave me back there. I've never been kissed like that before." He reached out and stroked her hair, tucking one stray curl behind her ear.

Tessa jerked away when his finger grazed her ear. "Do you mind? I'm trying to drive." She spared Rob a quick glare.

"Oh," he teased lightly, running one finger down her arm, "am I distracting you?" His voice was soft and husky. "Does my touch arouse you? Do you want me?" He stroked her arm again, his touch lingering on the curve of her elbow. Gooseflesh rose under his touch and he smiled at her. "It arouses me," he confessed. "Just being near you makes me hot. That kiss made me rock hard." He shifted in his seat, one hand tugging the legs of his pants away from his groin. "Tessa, I've wanted you for so long. I need you. Badly. Now." He groaned softly. "I don't care who you are dating. I need you. Hard and fast. I need to be buried in your hot wet sheath."

His bold, sexual words were uncharacteristic of her reticent friend, and were like pouring gasoline of the fire of Tessa's arousal. She flushed, grew hot and wet, and her nipples pebbled into tight nubbins that tested the strength of her thin t-shirt. The soft caress of his fingers on her arm made her long to feel those fingers on other parts of her body. Everywhere. She wanted him too, she realized. She wanted him with a desperate driving need that was beginning to distract her from the road.

"Damn," she whispered, glaring when he laughed. "Shut up," she ordered, "or I'm gonna pull over and fuck you right here." She turned on her indicator and eased into the off-ramp lane. "Ten minutes, keep your big mouth shut for ten minutes." She spared him a quick glare. "When we get to your house, I'm going to make you regret those words."

"Tessa, I dare you." He laughed again and grinned at her. "Unless you walk away and never come back, there is no way in the world that I will regret telling you how much I need you."

Rob popped open the front door, threw his kit into the corner and dragged Tessa into his arms as he kicked the front door shut. "You have one chance," he warned her. "I'm giving you one chance to tell me to back off before I make love to you."

Tessa wrapped her arms around Rob, looked up at him and said, "Make love to me, Rob. I need you. Bad." She kissed him on the chin, exploded from his arms, and shot up the stairs.

Five seconds later, her words registered and Rob bolted into action. Even though he took the stairs two at a time, by the time he arrived in the bedroom, Tessa lay on his bed; arms cupped behind her head, her clothing discarded except for matching white lace panties and bra. She gave him a big smile. "Come on, Soldier Boy. It's time I thanked you for serving." She gave him a big wink and twisted her hips enticingly.

"Geez Tessa." Rob groaned and reached for the top button on his camouflage shirt. He fumbled hurriedly with the fastenings until Tessa spoke.

"Go slow. Strip for me," she whispered. "Tease me a little, I want to enjoy every second of this." She laughed when he blushed from the collar of his shirt to the roots of his blonde brush cut. His blue eyes sparkled and he stilled his motions. His blush was so cute, so endearing, that she wanted to pull him into her arms and cuddle him close.

Tessa wiggled upwards on the bed to lean against the pillows propped against the carved headboard. Her eyes widened as he eased forward to stand closer to the bed, his fingers slowly unbuttoning his shirt. One button, then two, and the green khaki of his undershirt came into view. "An undershirt?" Tessa moaned. "I want you naked."

Rob blushed again and pulled his shirt from the waistband of his pants, making quick work of the remainder of the buttons and casting it aside. He settled his hands on the buckle of his belt and paused to look down at her. "Tell me what you want."

"Take your pants off soldier." Tessa wiggled on the bed, her hips moving restlessly. "Get naked for me. I need -" Her words trailed off as Rob's fingers slowly, carefully, undid his belt and eased it free of the belt loops before dropping it carelessly aside. "More," her voice squeaked and he slipped his pants button free and slid the zipper down slowly.

Electric heat zinged through Tessa and she writhed on the bed. "Yes," she whispered her voice soft and harsh. She cleared her throat and spared a glance for Rob's face. "Oh my god," she cried, "you're blushing." She sounded contrite and bounced to her knees to assist him. To her surprise, Rob backed away.

Still blushing furiously, he said, "You asked for this. Let me give it to you." He punctuated his words by dropping his fatigues and stepping clear of them. Two quick motions freed him from his socks and he looked back up at her. "Lay down," he commanded, his hands toying with the hem of his t-shirt.

Tessa scurried to obey and wriggled back to her seat at the headboard, eyes wide and focused on Rob's every move. Oh god, she thought, would kill her with his slow motions. She bit her lip and watched him ease his shirt higher and higher until he pulled it over his head, briefly covering his grin. He tossed the shirt at her and stood there, hands at his sides, that smug, slightly embarrassed grin on his face and let Tessa look her fill. He was divine standing there in nothing but his boxers.

Tessa clutched the shirt to her chest and sucked in a deep breath as she admired him. Damn, the shirt smelled like Rob. That hint of man and the overtones of his spicy aftershave. She inhaled again, drawing his enticing scent deeper into her lungs, surrendering to its power to arouse her even further. Licking suddenly dry lips, Tessa looked Rob up and down. He wasn't tall, he was five-nine, but he was nicely built. He worked hard in the military and it kept him fit and strong. His muscles rippled with tension as he stood there, submitting to her appraisal.

"Oh god," she begged, "bring that delectable body over here. I need to touch you." She swallowed hard when he took a slow step, bringing him back to the side of the bed.

"What do you want Tessa?" he asked in a low purr, his voice husky and teasing, hand caressing his abdomen just above the waistband of his shorts.

"Come here, Rob," she begged. "I need to touch you. I need you to touch me." Arousal shivered through her at the sound of her own pleas. How could she have gone so long without seeing this man? How had she missed his perfection, his delightful masculine presence and wicked smile? How could she have been oblivious to his importance in her life? When had he changed from childhood friend to…more?

Slowly he crawled across the bed, his eyes filled with happiness and sparkling with arousal. Rob leaned over Tessa and she relaxed into the pillows, welcoming his slow, teasing advance. He paused over top of her, his legs straddling hers, his arms braced by her shoulders. He looked down at her and smiled the slowest, sexiest smile she had ever seen.

"I've been waiting since you were sixteen for this. Ten long years," he whispered and eased himself down onto her, his mouth meeting hers and swallowing Tessa's startled response.

Chapter Five

Rob's words surprised Tessa, and before she could find the words to question him, her thoughts evaporated under the tender assault of his mouth. His lips caressed and tasted hers, pressing softly, then more firmly, his tongue dancing on her lips before edging sideways, kissing his way to her ear. His touch was light, hardly more than a whisper of a caress, but left a trail of tingling fire in its wake. Tessa wiggled against him, her arms drawing Rob down closer, bringing their bodies together. Rob rolled slightly to one side, pulling her gently with him, so she was cocooned in his embrace, one arm under her neck, the other around her waist.

He kissed her softly, slowly, on the mouth, his tongue delving in to caress the inside of her lip before retreating. He drew her bottom lip into his mouth and sucked on it gently, the action soft and teasing while his hand danced up and down her side, stroking and touching.

Frissons of electricity danced across her skin and Tessa moaned in delight. His hand cupped her breast, thumbing her nipple through the thin lace of her bra. "Oh my," she whispered breathlessly, arching her back, pressing forward, moulding her body to Rob's. "Oh, you feel so nice against me," she murmured.

His muscles were like warm, velvet-covered steel under Tessa's fingers as she explored his body, the bulk of his biceps, the curve of his back, the corded steel of his legs. She shifted and squirmed, trying to

55

reach all of him at once, trying to memorize the luscious landscape that she had been oblivious to for so long.

Tessa's skin burned under the soft caress of Rob's hands and mouth. "More," she begged, "I need you now." She felt, rather than heard Rob's chuckle as his hands slowed and stilled.

"Sweetheart, I'm gonna take my time loving you. I've waited far too long to rush this." He slid his fingers across her belly, inching slowly toward the curve of her breasts.

"Rob, please. I need you now." Oh god, she was going to die if she didn't have him soon. How could she go from oblivious to him as a lover to desperation so quickly? Tessa realized that she didn't care. She wanted him now. Hard and fast. Wiggling out of his embrace, she knelt on the bed and quickly stripped herself of her bra and panties and started tugging Rob's underwear off. "Naked, now!" she growled when he resisted her efforts to disrobe him.

"Slow and teasing." He pulled away, yanking his underwear from her grasp. "I'm going to memorize every inch of your body; with my hands, with my eyes, but mostly with my tongue." He pushed her down onto her back, his eyes travelling over every inch of her naked body. "Damn, you are even sweeter than I thought you would be. Your waist is so small." His fingers lingered at the dip in her waist, his thumb slowly stroking the flat plains of her stomach.

"Your hips are soft and luscious." He trailed his tongue across the curve of her hip and licked his way upwards. His hand and mouth stilled, just below the curve of her breasts.

Tessa moaned. Her skin was on fire, she was dying for his touch, to feel him inside her, filling her and pleasing her. Goose flesh covered her skin, her nipples beaded into hard pebbles when she felt his hand cup the underside of her left breast even as his tongue trailed upwards, slowly inching its way toward her nipple. When his lips closed over it, moisture flooded her pussy and she bucked against him. Her hands flew to his head, cupping it, guiding his mouth.

"Suck," she pleaded, and sighed gratefully when he obeyed. Slowly he increased the suction on one nipple, as he rolled the other hard nubbin between his thumb and forefinger. "Harder." The word was a whispered plea. Jarring tingles of electricity coursed through her, bringing her body to life, lodging in her core. She moistened and flowered, her body eager to welcome Rob into her warmth, desperate for completion, for the bliss of orgasm.

"I can't wait," she cried aloud.

"Yes, you can," Rob teased her, his words muffled by the nipple clenched lightly between his teeth. He trailed his hand down her belly, pausing to rub small circles at the juncture of her thighs. "Oh," he said in surprise, "you're so smooth. No bristles?" Tessa grunted a response, and bucked against him, urging him lower, silently pleading him to caress lower, to touch her femininity and stroke her clit.

"Patience." Rob trailed his fingers over Tessa's thighs, up over her hip and back down to caress the firm curve of her outer thigh. "Your skin is so soft. I love the way it twitches under my hand." He scraped his fingernail teasingly across her belly, and laughed when it undulated in his wake.

"Please." Tessa bucked and wiggled, her hands stroking, learning, memorizing Rob's shoulders, arms chest and back. His back was like molten iron; hot, solid and shifting with each caress. She trailed her fingers down his back, shifting slightly so she could reach the taut curve of his buttocks. "Mm."

Rob's hands slid down her belly, grasping her waist and pulling her flat onto the bed. "Don't move," he murmured against her breast before drawing the nipple back into his mouth and sucking firmly. He teased one nipple with his left hand, his right-hand dancing briefly against her naked mound before sliding lower to test her readiness.

Tessa twitched as his fingers stroked briefly over her clit before sliding lower and delving into her core. Rob slid the tip of one finger inside her and drew it back out slowly. With deliberate, slow motions, he eased it back inside and out again, each stroke deeper than the last. When he was fully inside, he withdrew once more and stroked her clit, moistening it, before delving back inside again. In and out he went, penetrating her slowly, then caressing her clit with small slow circles, teasing and arousing her.

Tessa arched upwards, but Rob's fingers gripped her shoulder, holding her down against the mattress while his fingers tortured her pussy, and his mouth worshipped her breasts. Shivers danced over her skin, her nipples peaked harder, and her pussy grew moister under his tender assault. She clutched his head to her breast, urging him on, directing his ministrations as she writhed under his expert caress.

Her eyes drifted shut as he slid a second finger inside her moist core, his fingers pumping in and out, his palm rubbing slow circles on her clit. His tongue matched those motions, licking slow circles around and around her nipple. Rob slowly increased the speed of his motions, his fingers moving faster and faster, flying in and out as Tessa moved restlessly against them. When she groaned low in her throat and arched upward, he slipped his fingers free and let them rest motionless outside her body. It flitted through her mind that this was more than casual sex; Rob was making love to her, worshipping her body like a man in love. It was a heady feeling.

"Not so fast," he warned. "It's not time yet." He laughed at her groan of despair.

He kissed his way across her breast, trailing his mouth to plant soft moist kisses on her belly and the curve of her hips. When her frantic motions slowed, Rob eased his fingers inside her and renewed his loving assault. Each time she neared her peak, Rob backed off. Instead he teased and caressed her, keeping her on the edge of bliss without taking her over the precipice.

"Please Rob," Tessa begged. "I can't wait any longer." She grasped his wrist and urged him on, helping him find the motion she needed so desperately. "Please, just one orgasm?"

"Are you sure?" he teased, looking down at her, his heart clutching at the sight of her, her lips parted, breathing heavily, bucking and writhing against him. She was beautiful. Darned if he didn't love her.

"Yes," Tessa groaned. "Please."

"Just one," Rob whispered against the curve of her neck as he increased the speed of his motions, driving his fingers deeper and deeper, harder and faster into her.

Waves of arousal coursed through Tessa's body, lodging in her core, driving her higher and higher, removing all thought, erasing everything except the sensations Rob was giving her as he pushed her closer and closer to the edge, and at long last driving her over the edge in an explosion of light, sensation and color.

"Oh, oh, oh," she panted breathlessly against his mouth as Rob's lips clamped down on hers, swallowing the sounds of her pleasure. Slowly easing back down to earth, to reality, she whispered, "Oh my," her voice rising sharply as Rob suddenly increased the tempo of his caresses, once again sending Tessa into a spiral of sensation, driving her quickly toward a second, then a third peak.

Several minutes later, Tessa returned to reality. Blinking frantically, she tried to focus on Rob's grinning face. "Oh my," she whispered again, "thank you."

Rob laughed. "You're thanking me?"

"Those were incredible orgasms." She smiled up at him. "But it's my turn now." Wiggling out from under him she corrected, "Actually, it's your turn." She quickly divested him of his boxers, kneeled between his legs and took his cock into her hand. "What have we here?" she teased, flicking her thumb back and forth across its purple head, sweeping up the pearly drop at its tip. Tessa looked up at Rob and licked her lips. "I think I need to taste this." Without breaking eye contact, she flicked her tongue over his glans and cupped his balls in one hand.

"Damn," Rob growled with a smile, his eyes drifting shut. "You are nasty."

Smiling broadly, Tessa pumped her hand up and down his shaft and licked her way slowly around and around his head before opening her mouth wide and taking the head of his cock into her mouth. His cock was big enough that she almost couldn't stretch wide enough to take him into her mouth. It was tough, but she managed it, and managed to lick the head of his cock with short flicking strokes until he bucked under her assault.

Opening her mouth as wide as she could, Tessa eased her mouth down over his cock, and began pumping up and down slowly, teasing him with her lips, her tongue dancing over the tip each time she drew back, and pressing against his length each time she took him back inside her mouth. He was wide, too wide to allow her to engulf his entire length. Tessa felt his hands on her head, not guiding her, not controlling her, just touching. Rob's legs quivered against her knees, his fingers clenched and unclenched in her hair. His entire body twitched with the effort to stay still, to not overpower her and take her mouth roughly.

His breathing grew ragged and uneven. "Enough," he groaned, pushing her away. "I can't take any more of this. I need to be inside you."

"But I'm not finished yet." Tessa laughed. "You are too delicious for me to quit now." In spite of her words she allowed Rob to ease her onto her back and squirmed around a bit until he was centered between her thighs. She needed this too, needed Rob inside her as much as he needed to be there.

"Condom," Tessa urged. "Get a damned condom." He extracted one from the bedside table and she slid it onto him and pulled him close.

Smiling up at Rob, Tessa arched upwards when his hand cupped her breast and his mouth lowered to capture hers. He kissed her gently, deeply as he shifted between her legs until his cock bumped against her opening. She twitched her hips a little until he was perfectly seated against her, tilted her pelvis up, and slid down on the bed a fraction of an inch. The tip of Rob's cock slipped inside her moist opening.

A breathless sigh escaped Tessa. He was so hot, so hard, and she was wet and ready for him. When Rob didn't move, she bucked her hips a little. "Come on, what are you waiting for?" she pleaded with him.

Rob grunted. "I am savoring the moment." He looked down at her and smiled.

"Well, savor it from the inside," she demanded, thrusting her hips upwards, her moist core engulfing just a bit more of him. She bucked again, and again, each upward thrust taking him deeper.

"You...don't...play...fair." He growled and thrust hard, seating himself fully into her moist heat. "I wanted to savor this." His hips thrust down against her, pinning her tight against the bed, preventing Tessa from moving. He nibbled her earlobe and flexed his groin muscles, making his cock twitch.

"Not fair," Tessa groaned, trying in vain to move her hips. She scraped her fingernails lightly across his shoulders. He flexed again, and she sucked in a breath. He smelled divine. What was it about the fresh scent of a freshly sweating man that was so arousing? She licked a droplet of sweat that was inching its way down his neck. "Mm."

He flexed again and she clamped down on his cock, clenching tight with her pussy muscles. He groaned, "you are so tight, and wet and hot." He flexed, and Tessa squeezed tight. "Don't squeeze like that," Rob panted, rising up, bracing his hands beside her shoulders.

"Don't twitch," Tessa countered with a laugh and another squeeze. "Put that magnificent tool to work."

With a low moan, Rob slowly eased his hips back, withdrawing partially and with a wicked grin, eased back inside. Slowly, he eased in and out, each stroke longer than the previous, until he was moving his entire length in and out.

"Oh," Tessa groaned. "That's so good, right there." Tilting her pelvis down Tessa twitched under him. Rob's motions were slow and methodical. Tessa smiled at the deep look of concentration on his face. "What" she asked breathlessly "are you thinking?"

"Waiting," he grunted, the motions of his hips speeding up. "Hurry."

Tessa laughed. It had been a long time since she had laughed during sex. What was it about Rob that was so much fun? Tingles raced over her body in the wake of her laughter, heat suffused her face, her chest and inched its way lower. She felt herself moisten further as her orgasm approached, her pussy spasmed on the brink.

"Stop ... clenching," Rob growled.

"I'm not," Tessa said, even as she felt a spasm of orgasm tightening her pussy around him. "Can't help it." Thrusting her hips upward she bucked against him, urging Rob on, hurrying his pace, driving her own orgasm closer.

"Yes, you are." He ground the words out through gritted teeth, his thrusts frantic. "Damn." His toes clenched, the tension rising up through his calves and thighs to his ass and groin. "Sorry," Rob grunted, pumping hard and fast as his orgasm overtook him and he exploded inside the hot clenching warmth of Tessa's pussy.

"Oh." Shock waves of arousal coursed through Tessa as Rob's release triggered her own. With one final buck of her hips, she exploded over the edge into pure bliss.

Tessa came back to reality, the sounds of their breathing harsh in her ears. Her heart pounded, her skin tingled. "That was fabulous. Thank you." She grinned at Rob as he looked down at her. He kissed her on the forehead and rolled off to lie beside her.

"Tessa, Kiddo; that was better than fabulous."

"Worth waiting ten years for?" she quipped, rolling over to face him.

"Danged right." He agreed instantly, tugging on a curl of her hair. "You look so hot with your hair messed up like this." He tugged another wayward curl, tucking it behind her ear. "You have that just screwed look." Rob rolled onto his side, facing Tessa, his lips finding hers.

"Just screwed? I believe the expression is just fucked. I love that you don't swear."

"Ha. I swear. I just try not to swear in front of ladies." He kissed her again and slowly pulled back. "You know, if I wasn't starving, I would be all over you right now."

"I lose out to food?" she teased, smacking him lightly on the arm. "I am devastated." She rolled away from him pretending to pout.

"How about if I make us something to eat?" he cajoled, stroking the soft curve of her neck.

"You've been out of the country for six months. Exactly what are you planning to feed me?" She threw a mocking glance over her shoulder.

"I might have some bread in the freezer ..." He traced a finger slowly down her spine.

"Maybe a glass of water too?" Tessa couldn't quite keep the laughter from her voice. "Have you got anything to go with that bread? Maybe some butter?"

"I think," he said, rising from the bed, "that I might be able to find some eggs, a couple of steaks, hash browns and freshly squeezed orange juice. If," he bowed low, "that will suit your majesty."

"Okay, that's just mean. Teasing me like that. You know that I'm a carnivore. Don't ever offer steak unless you mean it." She threw herself across the bed at him with a growl.

Stepping back hands in the air he surrendered. "Honest ma'am. I have steak, and eggs. All of it." Laughter filled his voice. "I have a house keeper. She cleans for me, and when I am away, Nora watches the house. I sent her a food order last week. The steaks should be in the fridge already. Of course," he added plaintively, "they were supposed to be my supper. And I spent eons on a plane with only airline food to sustain me." He huffed out an aggrieved breath and picked up his underwear. "I will attempt to survive, and share with you." Stepping into his underwear he headed out the door. "Have a shower and meet me downstairs in ten minutes. I'll make coffee."

Damn, she thought, moving toward the en-suite bathroom. He makes love like a god, cooks and makes coffee. Does it get any better than this? She thought she could fall for him. And after all this time too. She shook her head and turned on the shower. Catching sight of herself in the mirror she groaned. "This is the just fucked look? Holy hell, I look like I was caught in a windstorm. The man is out of his mind." Peace and contentment washed over her as she stepped into the shower. Life was good.

♥♥♥

Travel mugs of coffee in their hands, Tessa and Rob settled themselves onto a park bench three blocks from Rob's house.

"That was the best brunch I've had in years." Tessa groaned. "I ate way too much and I'm bloated." She rubbed her belly and leaned against him. "Thanks."

"You're welcome." He reached out and rubbed her belly. "I'll still love you when you're fat from all my excellent cooking."

Love? Yikes! Tessa went stiff beside him, and pulled away from the arm he slipped around her. He loved her? What the hell? Her mind exploded with contradictory thoughts. She could almost believe his words, but her ex had sworn he loved her too, and look where that had led her.

She wanted to snuggle in closer to Rob. She wanted to run, laugh and cry. She didn't know what she wanted. She bubbled with happiness and was scared stiff all at once.

"Fat?" she finally managed to squeak out, ignoring his declaration. "You think I'm fat? I'll have you know that I do kick boxing three times a week. I am as fit as a fiddle," she declared defiantly.

Rob turned her to face him. "You are perfect." he declared solemnly. "And I scared you. It's too soon to tell you that I love you." He stood and paced back and forth in front of Tessa. "But it's true. I've loved you for years. I couldn't keep quiet any longer."

He smiled down at her. "I don't expect you to feel the same way. I just wanted you to know." He grabbed her hand and tugged her to her feet. "So, quit worrying and just be who you are. No pressure on you, but no more denial by me. I love you, Tessa Dupree, and there's not a damned thing you can do about it. Race you to the swings." He dropped his cup and took off at a dead run across the park.

"Holy fuck," she whispered, dropped her mug beside his and took off after him. "What do I do now?"

She caught up to Rob quickly, not even caring that he let her catch him and tackled him from behind, dragging him to the ground. "You are dead, Gallagher." She wiggled her fingers under his shirt and started tickling him.

Rob bucked under her, throwing Tessa off, and rolled on top of her. "Ha. Not ticklish," he declared. "But you started this war." He quickly found the sensitive spot at her waist and attacked mercilessly until Tessa was wracked with gales of helpless laughter.

"Mercy," she panted. "Uncle." She tried in vain to dislodge him. "You … win." Panting and groaning she tried to call him off.

"What's my forfeit?" he asked. "If I win this battle, I deserve a prize." He tickled some more.

"Anything. Sto-op," Tessa pleaded breathlessly.

"Anything?" he asked deviously, not stopping his assault.

"Y-y-yes. Just stop." Rob's fingers stilled then their motion turned the assault into a caress, so light as to be almost unnoticeable. Tessa's skin twitched. "Oh my," she panted, and punched him lightly on the arm. "Bastard."

Rob laughed at her and kissed her on the nose. "Kiddo, you are my slave for the rest of the day. That's my forfeit." He rose to his feet pulling her with him. "Now, I need a fresh coffee. Your first task as my slave is fresh coffee and a massage on the bearskin rug by the fire."

"You're going to massage me? Sweet deal." She laughed.

"No," he replied slowly. "You are going to massage me."

"Damn. I was hoping ..." she trailed off. "Where did you get that bear skin from anyway? It's not exactly politically correct you know?" They picked up their discarded mugs and started back toward the house.

"It was my grandfather's. Back when they had the farm, the bear was attacking the cows so he shot it. They preserved the skin and fed the meat to the pigs." He shrugged. "I inherited it when he passed on. I loved playing hunter as a kid, stalking and killing it." He laughed at his own youthful antics. "It's a good memory for me."

"Wow," Tessa said quietly. Her heart filled with something soft and she felt warm and happy all over.

They arrived home to the ringing of the telephone. "You keep a landline when you're only home a couple of weeks of the year?" She asked as he picked it up. She grinned at his chagrined shrug and headed to the kitchen to start a fresh pot of coffee, leaving him privacy for his call. He found her there a few minutes later, sitting at the table, cup cradled in her hand.

She waved toward another cup on the table. "Strong and black, just the way you like it, oh Master of my day."

He sipped the coffee and sighed. "Nirvana," he declared. "You have any plans for later?"

"Well, I seem to recall something about a massage, but other than that? No. My day is yours and I don't work until the day after tomorrow. Why?" She resisted the urge to ask who was on the phone, knowing it was none of her business, but she was still curious.

"That was my neighbor on the phone. And you don't have to leave when the phone rings. I have no secrets from you." Rob smiled at her, "None. Anyway, he wanted to know if I could come to a barbecue tonight. Kind of a welcome back thing." He shrugged. "I said yes and I would like to take you with me, if you want to come." His voice held a hint of question and vulnerability.

"Hmm," she teased, "will there be meat there? This isn't a veggie thing is it? I need my protein. When do we leave?"

"Mitch said to show up around four. Some beers, football, a barbecue. I guess he's inviting most of the neighborhood."

"You know your whole neighborhood?" she asked, thinking of her own quiet apartment, feeling just a bit envious. Some things about suburban life just couldn't be found in a high-rise.

"Come on, Tessa, there are only nine houses on the cul-de-sac. We're all friends. We watch out for each other, party together, that kind of stuff. There are six couples, three single guys including me and about nine hundred kids. Do you still want to go?"

"What the hell, why not?" Maybe this would be a proving ground for her, Tessa thought. She was feeling something new and nice here. Whatever was between her and Rob deserved some exploration, she needed to know where it was going as much as she needed to know just what it was she was feeling. "I'm going to have to go home and change." She gestured to the grass stains on her jeans. "Is this a fancy thing?"

"Definitely not, it's shorts and a t-shirt for me. Dress casual. Bring your swimsuit, preferably your bikini." He waggled his eyebrows at her. "One second thought, bring a large, one piece, all covering, bathing suit. Mitch and Pete are bachelors. I don't want them ogling you. I'll drive you home to change."

Pete? Her heart gut clenched at the thought. What are the odds that it would be the same man? None, Tessa. She laughed at herself. There isn't a chance in a million that it would be the same Peter. He was a one-night stand, and even on her worst days, Tessa knew her luck wasn't bad enough, or was that good enough, that he would show up in her life again.

Tessa laughed at him. "Bikini it is and I'll drive myself. I brought you home. Remember? Will this run late?"

"Yeah, typically they do. But we can leave anytime you want. No obligation. If you want, bring your pajamas. You can sleep here." He blushed. "In the spare bedroom if you want."

Tessa rounded the table and straddled his lap, grinding down against him. "Done with me already," she quipped, kissing him long and deep, not stopping until she felt his cock rise against her ass. "Here I thought I was going to get me some on a bearskin rug. Damn." She slid off his lap and sashayed to the door.

"Forget the pajamas," Rob groaned, following her. "You'll be naked in my bed."

"Naked? Won't I get cold?"

"I will keep you warm enough to sleep, *IF* I let you sleep at all. And that's a big if."

Katie O'Connor

Chapter Six

Clicking the button to activate her blue-tooth, Tessa turned the corner onto the main street to take her home. "Call Shayla." She tapped her fingers on the steering wheel while she waited to be connected. "Be home, be home. Answer the damned phone."

Shayla's old style, desk top answering machine kicked in. "Heya. This is Shayla. I'm not here, leave a message."

"Pick up the damned phone," Tessa ordered, hoping that her best friend was screening her calls. "Now! I need you, woman." The phone clicked in her ear.

"What's the emergency? I was painting my toe-nails." Shayla's voice was loaded with laughter.

"Oh god," Tessa groaned. "I've messed up big time." She flicked her turn indicator on and waited for a chance to merge into the next lane.

"What is it this time? You pick up another stranger at the bar?" Her voice was mocking and she laughed aloud.

"Worse. I slept with Rob." Tessa blurted out, completely ignoring her friend's sarcasm.

"Get the fuck out! You did not." Shayla laughed.

"I did, I picked him up at the airport, drove him home and jumped his bones. What the hell am I going to do now?" The words came out in a rush.

"Get your ass over here, I'll call the girls and we can strategize this." That was the beauty of Shayla and the rest of their friends; it didn't matter what the crisis was, they all jumped at the first call and came together to rescue each other. "Was he good?"

"I don't have time to wait for the girls. This is just you and me. He was amazing," Tessa sighed blissfully. "I'm almost home, meet me at my place."

"As good as your bar-man?" Shayla asked lightly.

"Yes. What the hell do I do now? He told me he loves me."

"The bar-guy?"

"No idiot. Rob." Tessa swore a blue streak. "He said he's loved me for ten years. We're going to a party today, to meet his neighbors. This is serious. What the hell do I do?"

"Go to the party, see what happens?" Shayla asked.

"What about Peter?"

"Who the hell is Peter? Oh, the bar-guy. You never did tell us his name. What about him? You don't even have his number?"

"But I slept with him two nights before I slept with Rob. I'm turning into a slut." Tessa wailed as she shoulder-checked before switching lanes. Her emotions felt like Ping-Pong balls rattling around her chest, upsetting her stomach.

"So, tell Rob you don't want to go to the party. Cut him off before this goes any further," Shayla advised in her usual no-nonsense way. "Chalk him up as your second one-night stand."

"But what if I love him?" Her voice trailed off and she whispered the last two words. Everything was always black and white for Shayla; it was part of what made her a good sounding board; well, that and the fact that she never hesitated to give her opinion, even when you didn't ask.

"What? You're breaking up. I can hardly hear you. Jesus, Tessa, speak up."

"What if I love him?" Tessa shouted. "I am so screwed."

"So, forget the bar-guy then."

"But it was some of the best sex I've ever had. I've never connected with anyone like that. Except Rob," she amended. "I mean it was electric, crazy, and fabulous."

"With Rob?"

"With both of them." Tessa groaned. "Pay attention. Dammit."

"I am paying attention. You're rattling on a thousand miles an hour. Tess, baby, you aren't making any sense. Pick a direction. Bar guy was probably only good because of the chance of getting caught. Forget him. You've known Rob for years. He's a great guy."

Tessa pulled into her parking stall, pulled on the emergency brake and shut it off. "I'm here. Get your ass down to my apartment. I've only got about ten minutes before I have to go back to Rob's for the party."

By the time Tessa arrived at her third-floor door, Shayla was leaning casually against the wall, tapping her freshly painted toes impatiently. Tessa smiled at her curvaceous brunette friend. "Thank god you're here."

"Spill the beans. And start at the beginning. This whole sordid story has me confused out of my mind." She followed Tessa into the apartment and into the bedroom, throwing herself on the bed and fluffing her shoulder length, dark-brown hair. "Shoot."

"Okay, so I already told you, I met Peter at The Pub the other night. We had sex in the parking lot." Tessa groaned and covered her eyes. "God, I can't believe I did that. But we connected immediately. It was like I've known him all my life. And the sex was fucking amazing."

"But you didn't get his number, or give him yours? I still don't get that. I've never passed up a chance to get a hot guy's number, or to give him mine." She winked outrageously.

"Yeah well, a cop kind of interrupted us." Tessa flushed beet red and started digging in her closet for her overnight bag. "We left as fast as we could. No numbers. And he still has my panties in his pocket."

Shayla bolted upright, her braless breasts bouncing beneath her tank top and her green eyes sparkling with mirth. "You didn't tell us that part." She laughed with glee. "He kept your underwear? No fucking way."

"Way," Tessa mumbled from the closet.

"This just gets better and better." Shayla rubbed her hands together with glee.

"Don't you dare tell anyone else," Tessa warned. "Promise me."

"Promise?" she asked skeptically. "Not a chance in hell, Tessa. This is too good to keep a secret. But I'll try," she added in a conciliatory fashion. "But really, could you keep this a secret for the girls if our roles were reversed?"

"No. Dammit, dammit, dammit. What do I do?"

"So, Rob loves you? When did that happen? You must be one hell of a fuck."

"Ha ha." Tessa couldn't help but smile at the teasing. That was her favorite thing about Shayla. The girl pulled no punches and they had the kind of relationship where they could say anything without risking alienating each other.

"How long have we known Rob?" Shayla asked.

"Since grade six. And he said he fell in love with me when I was sixteen. My god, can you imagine? I had no idea." She rooted through her lingerie drawer, extracting a black and hot pink teddy combo. "What about this?" She threw it in the bag without waiting for an answer.

"Okay, so clearly you're going back to Rob's and you intend to sleep with him again. So, you're done with bar-guy?"

"Peter, his name is Peter. What are the odds that I'll ever see him again?" Tessa spared a glare for her friend, who laughed at her. "I don't know what to do about Rob; I don't know what we have. It's weird, it's good. But what if it turns to crap?" She swore loudly as she stripped off yesterday's clothing.

"Damn you are hot," Shayla declared. "No wonder Rob's in love with you. Look at that body." Shayla studied Tessa from head to toe, enjoying the view of Tessa's tight, fit, naked body.

"Shayla! Pay attention here. I've got issues."

"I am paying attention, to that fine, sexy body of yours. Too bad you're not bi." She sighed. They had been over that ground a number of times, and no matter how many times they covered it, Tessa never strayed from her stance that she was straight. Shayla, on the other hand, was admittedly bi-sexual and loved to tease Tessa.

"Shayla!" Tessa barked and slipped into a red lace bra and panty set before digging out a pair of cut-offs. "What do I do?"

"Okay, all kidding aside. Go, spend more time with Rob and see where it goes. Forget bar-guy. Peter. Don't think about where it's going with Rob; just take it all one day at a time. Don't risk losing Rob over some mistaken worry. Just relax and enjoy it, whatever happens." She waggled her eyebrows suggestively.

"You really think it could work out?"

"I repeat," Shayla said, "take it one day at a time and see what happens. There's no sense worrying about things that might not happen. Rob isn't anything like your dickhead ex." Shayla picked up a jar of lotion and began smoothing it into her lightly tanned legs.

Tessa sucked in a deep breath and released it in a huff. "True, Rob's been my friend for years, and he has always treated me better than Rick did. Not that Rick treated me badly," she hedged.

Shayla quirked one eyebrow at her.

"How do you do that?" Tessa asked, trying, unsuccessfully, to raise one of her eyebrows. Her forehead scrunched up comically, in spite of the seriousness of their discussion. Without waiting for an answer, she continued talking. "Okay, so Rick was…"

"A dick? A prick? A complete and total asshole? A useless mother-fucker?" Shayla offered adjectives helpfully.

"Okay." Tessa sighed. "You're right. As always."

"Take it slow with Rob; forget bar-guy unless you run into him someplace. He was a one-night stand, a quickie, a fling…"

"All right already, I get the picture." She hugged Shayla close. "Thanks. I knew I could count on you to steer me straight." She returned to the dresser and pulled on a white knit tank top and short denim skirt. She threw jeans, runners, socks and a few other items into her overnight bag and stood for a minute, bikini in one hand, one-piece in the other. She glanced at one, then at the other before raising an inquiring eyebrow at her friend.

"The bikini, definitely." Shayla advised without being asked. "Drive him out of his mind. Let him know who is going to be boss in this relationship." She laughed.

"Is the bikini too much? This is a neighborhood thing."

"And?" Shayla winked. "Every guy wants to have the hottest girl in the place. Why would Rob be any different? Wear the bikini."

"But...oh, to hell with it." She tossed both swimsuits and a cover-up into the bag. "At this rate, I'll need a bigger suitcase."

Katie O'Connor

Chapter Seven

"You sure I look okay?" Tessa asked Rob, nervously running her hands down her denim skirt. This was a big step in their relationship. While they had known each other since they were children, Rob hadn't taken her to a party in his new neighborhood yet. The time they spent together was more one-on-one, or Rob joining Tessa and her friends. It hadn't been intentional; it was just the way their schedules meshed when he was on leave.

Rob leaned over and kissed her full on the mouth. "You look perfect no matter what you wear. Of course, I prefer you naked, Kiddo." He pulled open Mitch's front door and walked inside without knocking, leaving Tessa staring at his back. "Are you coming or what?" he quipped, grinning over his shoulder. "Stop worrying. You'll be great. Besides, I love you. Even if all my friends hated you, and they won't, I would still love you."

Tessa smiled at Rob and followed him inside. For as long as she had known him, he always knew just what to say to make her feel better, and strangely, this time, his declaration of love didn't make her feel uncomfortable. Instead, it filled her with reassurance and confidence.

Inside the house chaos reigned. Children were running everywhere, their laughter and shouts heralding their arrival and trailing behind them. Adult laughter echoed from the back of the house, and a small dog danced excitedly around Tessa's feet.

"Scotty, sit," Rob commanded and to Tessa's surprise the fluffy white bundle of energy immediately obeyed and sat quivering at their feet. "Good dog," Rob praised, leaning down to pet him. Scotty rolled over and lay on his back, panting while Rob tickled his belly.

The sound of galloping turned Tessa's attention to the back of the house. A German shepherd flew out of the kitchen and skidded to a stop at Rob's feet. Sitting patiently, it waited to receive its share of the attention.

"This behemoth," Rob said, patting the newcomer on the head; "is Alexis. She's about the biggest suck that ever lived."

"Uncle Rob, Uncle Rob." A chorus of voices distracted Tessa from the dogs. A small cluster of kids rushed at them, all clamoring for Rob's attention. They jumped and chattered excitedly, but were careful to avoid stomping on the dogs.

"Come play downstairs. We had to come in 'fore we got too much sun," said a blonde girl with pigtails. "What took you so long?"

"I was waiting for my friend." Rob told them, his voice patient and understanding. "This is my special friend Tessa. You be nice to her." One by one, he introduced them to Tessa, insisting that they shake her hand.

Introductions complete, the youngest, Amber, a four-year-old blonde with pigtails, took Rob by the hand and tried to lead him away, informing him in no uncertain terms that there was no way on earth they could solve the game level without his help, "cause nobody can beat the mean old dragon."

"Come on, Tessa. This won't take long." Giving in to the girls' urging, he followed the children from the room.

Tessa set her bag inside the closet and closed the door, preparing to follow them.

"Hi there," a deep masculine voice drawled. "We meet again."

Tessa turned to face the voice and found her gaze captured by a very attractive stranger. "I'm sorry, have we met?" She asked, not recognizing him. He was just over six feet tall and had short black hair. His khaki shorts revealed perfectly tanned, long legs. Broad shoulders stretched the cotton of his t-shirt and he smiled wickedly at Tessa. His feet were bare. When had bare feet become sexy? She wondered. And those eyes? Wow. They were like melted chocolate. If ever she had seen bedroom eyes, this man had them. Tessa wanted to melt into his eyes.

"Not exactly." The man grinned and winked at her. "Mitch Waters," he added, as if expecting his name to clear up the mystery of his identity.

Tessa offered her hand. "Tessa Dupree," she said. Mitch took her hand in his calloused one and shocked by the rush of arousal that swamped her from the simple contact, she almost jerked away. "I … I … um … I came with Rob," she stammered, disconcerted by the electricity of their touch.

"Rob?" he asked sounding surprised, but not releasing her hand. "I thought you were with Peter." He stroked the base of her thumb lightly, the soft contact sending shivers racing up her arm.

"Oh!" Tessa's eyes went wide with shock as his identity hit her. "Officer Waters?" She groaned in mortification. Here was the one person she could think of that she never, ever wanted to meet, and he was smoking hot. The universe definitely had a cruel streak.

"Yes ma'am," he drawled. "Pleased to meet you, to actually meet you that is. I didn't realize that you knew Rob *and* Peter."

"Um," Tessa stammered as she searched for a response. "I've known Rob for years. Peter and I met recently." It wasn't much of an explanation, but then, she really didn't owe this man an explanation, in spite of the awkwardness of their meeting and her attraction to him.

"Welcome to my home. Any friend of Rob and Peter's is a friend of mine." He smiled charmingly. "And, your secret is safe with me." Mitch winked suggestively and raised her hand to his lips.

His brash wink sent a shaft of desire zinging through Tessa and she blushed deeply. He brushed his lips softly, suggestively, across the back of her hand. Cool heat rushed up her arm, across her chest and down the other arm. Her nipples pebbled and she sucked in a startled breath.

Oh my, she thought. Surely, I'm not attracted to this brash man? But she was, and Tessa was too much of a realist to deny it, even to herself. But that didn't mean she had any intention of acting on it. Hell, she was in enough trouble already being attracted to two men at once. No way in hell was she going to add another man to complicate the mix even further.

"Come beautiful Tessa," Mitch tugged on her arm, leading her toward the noise at the rear of the house. "Let me introduce you to the gang. And I warn you, Peter is here."

"Shit," the word slipped out before Tessa could stop it.

Mitch looked at her and laughed. "Don't worry sweetie, he's discreet, he won't say anything to Rob, even though they've been friends for ages and are now neighbors. Neither will I."

Somehow, Tessa didn't find his words all that reassuring. Thankfully, Peter wasn't among the crowd gathered in the kitchen. She wasn't ready to face him. How the hell did she deal with having her one-night stand show up again? Even though Peter had been as sexy as sin, after her chat with Shayla, Tessa had concluded that that chapter was finished.

Mitch started his introductions. Most of the names passed in a blur, catching names the first time was not Tessa's strong suit. Three names did stick in her memory. Leaning against the counter with her arms around two men who were clearly twins, was a willowy blonde woman.

"Tessa meet Tammy, and her boy-toys, Daniel and Douglas."

Tammy extracted herself from the men, stepped forward and offered her hand to Tessa. "Don't let this jerk get to you," she advised. "Danny, Doug, and I have a different relationship. I couldn't choose between them, so I picked them both." She smiled and shrugged self-deprecatingly. "Don't let us make you uncomfortable, I know our lifestyle isn't for everyone. Let me get you a drink." She looked Tessa up and down. "White wine? No." She answered her own question. "Cooler or beer?" This time she waited for a response before digging into the cooler and extracting an icy beer and handing it to Tessa.

"Thanks." Tessa popped the top, took a deep swallow, moistening her suddenly dry throat. How could this woman be suggesting that one woman with multiple men in a serious relationship was possible? Could it really be that easy? The thought was made Tessa a bit uncomfortable. Conventional morals would say otherwise, but clearly the people gathered in Mitch's kitchen had no trouble with the idea. There seemed to be no judgement of the trio as far as Tessa could tell. At the very least, they showed no outward signs.

"I admit it," Mitch said, "I am jealous of you three. I've been single for too long now. I think it's about sixty-five years by actual count." He laughed when the entire room groaned. "What? I'm serious here. I'm just a lonely old bachelor, looking for love."

Tammy mock punched him in the arm. "You are married to your work. You're one hundred percent cop, through and through. You don't have the time or the inclination for a serious relationship. You specialize in frivolous blondes and one-night stands."

Mitch clutched his hands to his chest and tried his best to look forlorn before falling dramatically to his knees in front of Tessa. "But for this beauty, I would give it all up."

"Geez, Waters. Back off of my date." Rob's laughing drawl came from the doorway. Moving into the room, he slid his arm around Tessa's shoulders. "You, my friend," he pointed at Mitch, "will have to find your own girl. I've claimed this one."

Turning his attention to Tessa, Rob kissed her lightly on the cheek and said, "Gaming tragedy averted. I'm safe for ten minutes or so. Let's get some sun. I can catch up with these guys later." Grabbing a beer from the cooler, Rob led Tessa out into the back yard.

Tessa quickly scanned the yard, hoping against hope that Peter wasn't still at the party. Maybe something had come up and he had left. Relief filled her when she failed to find him among the crowd. People were milling about the large yard, some deep in conversation, and few men played catch with a football on the right side of the grass. Kids tumbled back and forth across the yard, playing on the small climbing structure or in the sandbox.

The left side of the yard was taken up by a hot tub and moderate sized swimming pool, complete with a teenage boy acting as life guard and an adoring girl standing with him. The air was redolent with the scent of sunscreen, chlorine and barbecue. Laughter and the bright sparkle of conversation filled the air. The late afternoon sun beamed down from a cloudless sky, giving the yard a festive, party atmosphere.

"Heads up," a voice shouted as an errant football came soaring in their direction. Pivoting in the direction of the voice, Rob caught the ball with ease and tossed it back.

"Rob. Glad you're back safe." The man tossed the ball to another player and jogged over to Rob and Tessa. He shook hands with Rob, drawing him into a quick, manly embrace before releasing him. "How long are you home for?"

"I've got three months back in town. But only three weeks of leave. I'll be in the office and doing some school visits while I'm here. It'll be nice to unwind and spend time with my special gal." Rob nodded toward Tessa. "Jake Young, this is Tessa Dupree. Tessa, Jake."

Tessa smiled at the tall, lean, blue eyed blond. Jake was very, very cute, practically drool-worthy. Tessa took his offered hand. "It's nice to meet you." For a moment, Tessa was afraid of being attracted to Jake too. Relief swamped her when their hands touched. Nothing. No tingles, no hot flashes, just pleasant hand-on-hand contact. Thank God, she thought. Being attracted to three men was enough. She smiled broadly at him.

"Rob, my man. Good to have you home." Peter's familiar voice came from behind Tessa, breaking off the conversation and sending a shiver of longing through her. How could a man's voice have such an instantaneous effect on her?

Damn, she thought, she had been hoping to pass the evening without seeing him. Ignoring the rush of pleasure at his voice, and the worry it caused, she pasted a smile on her face and turned around. Peter stood there, as handsome and attractive as the night they met. Her smile turned from forced to genuine and her eyes lit up. Yup, she thought, he's still hot. Those golden-brown eyes, the dark hair and his long lean runner's body, oh my. Oh yeah, she was still attracted to him, big time. Just looking at him swamped her with longing and she felt her nipples pebble and her pussy flower.

Rob and Peter shared a man-hug before Peter turned to Tessa. "Hey babe," he greeted her warmly, giving her a quick hug. "How are you?"

"You guys know each other?" Rob asked in a puzzled voice.

Tessa's mind flew into a panic. How the hell did she answer that? How did a person describe a one-night stand in a parking lot? Did she want Rob to know that Peter was the man she had told him about yesterday? And what about the crazy attraction for both of these men that was wracking her body right now? When did her life get so complicated?

"We met at The Pub a couple nights ago after the game." Peter told Rob, saving Tessa the discomfort of fabricating a story. "We really hit it off. We talked for hours." He flipped his arm around Tessa's shoulders. "Didn't we?" He asked, a hint of challenge in his voice, his eyes laughing. He spared Rob a challenging glance.

Tessa forced a laugh. "We did talk a long time," she hedged, looking at Peter with a hint of a glare. She slipped free of his arm with a quick smile, moving a fraction of an inch closer to Rob.

Tessa's gaze went from Peter to Rob and back again. They look like a couple of rutting moose, all animal testosterone and posturing. A small part of her was thrilled that they looked about ready to fight over her. But she wasn't a party favour to be wrangled over. How the hell had she gotten into this? She leaned a bit closer to the familiar comfort of Rob's side. He was her friend; she had known him for years. Granted, she hadn't realized how much he cared for her until recently. For a moment, she wondered how she could have been so oblivious to the depth of his caring. Peter on the other hand was an unknown. There ano denying that she had enjoyed his company, and they had shared some wickedly good sex. But did she really want these two men fighting over her? It was a bit of a thrill to be the center of attention.

Peter looked from Rob to Tessa and back again. His eyebrows pinched together. Rob slid a possessive arm around Tessa and pressed his lips tightly together.

The men stood there for several long moments glaring at each other. Then suddenly Peter smiled cunningly.

"I hope you have no claims on this woman," he challenged, "because I fully intend to see her again." Peter smiled down at Tessa, a flirtatious smile on his mouth and lighting his eyes.

Oh man, Tessa thought, did he have to throw down the gauntlet like that? What the hell was he thinking?

Rob looked from Tessa to Peter and back again. He gave her a long, slow, sexy smile. "I don't own her. We've been friends since grade school. But she is one special lady and I intend to see a lot of her." His glance at Peter was filled with warning, and his voice held a hint of menace. "If you hurt her, I'll kill you." He took a step forward, well into Peter's personal space and growled menacingly like an angry dog. "I warn you. Do...not...hurt...her. Because friend or not, I'll kill you."

"Fuck you Gallagher," Peter stepped in to chest bump Rob. "She's a big girl, she can take care of herself and date whoever the fuck she wants."

"Well, if you guys both get to date her, I do too." Mitch's voice startled Tessa.

"No fucking way," Rob and Peter barked in unison.

"Way," Mitch countered aggressively, glaring from one friend to the other.

She glanced around, surprised to discover that they had drawn a bit of a crowd and that the yard had grown quiet. She took a small step back from the trio of posturing men. What the hell had happened? Three men vying for her attention at once? Was it her, or was it nothing more than stupid macho posturing? She didn't know whether to run away screaming, or to egg them on. Part of her was nervous, but a much bigger part was thrilled. How the hell had this happened? For years she had dated the biggest asshole on earth, and now she had three decent guys chasing her. The universe made no sense.

She took a long slow drink of her beer, noticing how all three men's eyes followed her every move. Oh hell, they were all attracted to her, and as their eyes darkened with desire, she realized that she was hopelessly attracted to all of them. The question was where would it go from here? Was this all going to work out okay, or was this going to blow up big time? And how did she defuse the attention and distract everyone from viewing her personal life? She could live with being the center of attention for these three men, but she wasn't impressed to be the center of attention for the entire party.

She looked from Rob to Peter to Mitch and gave them each a smile. Then, without a word, she turned and walked away from them. Not sure where she was headed, she was desperate to escape the tension. She was pleased to see Tammy standing with a group of children across the yard, with a feeling of relief she joined them in a game of tag, leaving the men behind.

Behind her, the crowd slowly broke up and scattered into smaller groups around the yard. Relief flooded through Tessa, she didn't want to become the focus of gossip, let them find someone else to whisper about.

Hours later, Tessa slipped gratefully into the hot tub, a soft sigh of relaxation escaping her lips. The water was delightfully warm against her skin, the moon bright in the night sky and the yard blessedly silent. The water smelled vaguely of the bromine capsules used to treat it. Only a few people remained at the party, all of them inside the house. She closed her eyes, and leaned her head back, letting the warmth of the water flood through her, relaxing her tense muscles, helping her unwind. She knew that Mitch was inside with his guests, but wondered where Rob and Peter were, she hadn't seen them for a while. "Who cares?" She whispered to herself. "I just want to enjoy the water."

Tessa slid down in the hot tub until only her head remained above the water. "Damn." It had been one hell of a day. She had met so many people, and had rarely felt out of place. This tight knit group had a way of making a person feel welcome. There were nine houses on the cul-de-sac, which meant meeting seventeen adults and at least twenty kids and an untold number of dogs. That didn't even include the people she knew already. The entire day had been a kind of controlled pandemonium with lots of laughter and the occasional child in tears. Tessa sighed, thinking back on it. The day had been lovely, but it felt nice to relax and unwind. Her eyes drifted shut.

"Mind if I join you?" Mitch's quiet voice heralded his arrival.

"Mm," Tessa sighed and opened her eyes. "Not at all. After all, it is your hot tub." She watched him climb the stairs and step into the water. As he stepped into the tub, she looked him up and down; he did have a lovely body. He was just over six feet tall, with broad shoulders and a sculpted abdomen. His hair was dark, almost black and cut short, with little spikes up on top.

Tessa found her eyes drifting to the juncture of his thighs, and blushed to realize that she wondered how he was built there. Swallowing hard to moisten her suddenly dry throat, Tessa picked up her beer.

"See anything you like?" Mitch teased lightly. "I don't measure up to Peter and Rob," he confessed candidly, but without shame. "I know because we play lacrosse together. You can't hide anything in the showers."

Tessa choked, spitting beer into the tub and Mitch laughed at her.

"Well, I didn't want you to be disappointed later on." He winked and slid closer to her. "You should know I was serious earlier. I would like to take you out." When Tessa didn't answer, he continued. "I know you are already seeing my two best friends, but that doesn't concern me. If you are serious, or committed to one of them, all you have to do is say no and I'll leave you alone."

Tessa was stumped. Her thoughts raced around her brain trying to find an answer, a reason to deny this man. She came up dry. She felt something really special for Rob, but couldn't quite define it; and she had shared such electricity with Peter; and now here was Mitch, and just looking at him set her heart racing and her desire skyrocketing. For a girl who hadn't dated many men, all this attention felt like hitting the jackpot.

"Can I have time to think about this?" she asked at last.

"Take all the time in the world." Mitch grinned and leaned in to kiss her.

Mitch's lips collided with her own, sending shockwaves of desire coursing through her. His hand cupped the back of her head, burrowing in her hair, pulling her closer. Tessa sighed against his mouth and his tongue darted into the small opening between her lips and darted back out leaving her wanting more. Longing conflicted with shame that she wanted to kiss him while on a date with Rob. It was a mixed blessing when he leaned back against the edge of the tub and looked at her.

"You are beautiful, you know," Mitch advised her quietly. "There is just something so … so sensual and enticing about you. I can't put my finger on it, but I will." He took her beer and took a long slow pull of it. "And I don't think it stems from that hot scene I witnessed in that parking lot either." He shrugged and handed her back the beer. "At least not all of it."

Tessa stared at him in surprise. "Are you always this outspoken?" she asked, not sure if she approved or not.

"Pretty much." He shrugged and laughed. "Five years ago, I lost my sister to cancer. To this day I regret not telling her how much I loved her. The day she died is the day I swore never to keep my feelings confined." He brushed off Tessa's condolences. "I decided to speak up and let the chips fall where they may. That's why I told Rob and Peter, that they had competition for your affections. Something about you compels me and I'm not prepared to let you slip away without at least a shot at earning your affections. Are you okay with that?"

Tessa paused a moment before answering. "Honestly? I'm not sure how that makes me feel." A shiver went through her. Thrill or trepidation, she couldn't be sure. She didn't need another man in her life she was already juggling two and that was enough for any woman. But to include a third man was insanity, plain and simple insanity.

"And you talked to Peter and Rob about this?" Doubt filled her voice. "Somehow I can't see that." It didn't make sense that they would accept another man into the battle for her affections that had started earlier.

"We had a wicked argument downstairs earlier." He grinned unrepentantly. "I'm talking a screaming, hollering, hissy fit fight. We didn't quite come to blows, but it was damn close." He shrugged. "But we talked about what to do with you. I told you, I don't hide my feelings any longer. Not from family, not from friends, but certainly not from my best friends or the lovely lady we have all discovered. Ask them yourself." He advised as the door opened and the two other men, clad in swimsuits and carrying towels, stepped out onto the deck.

"Ask us what?" Peter demanded, dropping into the hot tub with a near-cannonball splash.

Tessa found she couldn't speak. Just how did one ask such a question without hurting the people you were asking, or sounding like a tramp for that matter? She licked her lips, grabbed her beer and took a gulp. Swallowing harshly, she searched for the right words. She looked from man to man to man. Not one of the three looked particularly happy; they must have had one hell of a row. Part of her wished she had witnessed the verbal battle, but most of her was glad it was over.

"She doesn't believe that I told you guys I was going to pursue her. Kind of a three-way competition." He looked from one friend to the other and shrugged.

Rob sighed. "Just when you finally dump your idiot man and I have a chance of showing you what you mean to me, these two morons want to hone in on you." He slid into the tub and draped one arm around Tessa.

"I, for one, am not a moron." Peter objected. "I gather the idiot is the ex you told me about the other night?" He glanced questioningly at Tessa.

"Yeah." She shrugged.

"Look guys don't leave her hanging," Mitch advised. "We've put our lovely Tessa in a tight spot here. Answer the question." His foot snaked out under the water to caress her calf lightly, sending a shiver up her leg in spite of the warmth of the water. Her heart raced at the simple contact.

"I don't like it," Rob grumbled. "But I don't own you. Yet! But I won't deny you your chance at happiness." He planted a quick kiss on her temple. "You mean that much to me. I've waited years for you to notice me and love me back. I'll wait longer, you are worth it." His words were conciliatory, but his tone told Tessa that he wasn't exactly pleased with the idea of sharing her. His possessiveness tickled her ego. It was nice to be wanted.

"I hate the idea," Peter said. "I fucking hate it with every fiber of my being. I thought we shared something special." He smiled crookedly at Tessa. "I had hoped to see more of you. Once I figured out how to find you, that is. And, if this is the only way to accomplish that, I guess I have to give in gracefully."

"Graceful? You call that graceful?" Rob teased. "You sound like a snivelling baby who can't get his way."

"Sounds like a case of sour grapes to me," Mitch added when Peter protested Rob's challenge. Then, like a group of high school kids, the fight was on. They bickered back and forth, teasing, name calling and insulting each other. Part of it was fun, but there were serious undercurrents to it as well.

A feeling of unease filled Tessa. She didn't feel comfortable where this was going. When they started splashing water at each other, Tessa had reached her limit. So much for a relaxing soak in the hot tub. Standing regally, she stepped from the tub and grabbed her towel. "Well guys, as much fun as this drenching is, I'm bushed. Rob, I'll see you when you get home." Scooping up her towel, she left them there, gaping after her.

Katie O'Connor

Chapter Eight

Tessa didn't bother to change. Instead she secured the towel around her waist, gathered up her clothing and her bag and headed across the street to Rob's house. After letting herself in, she took a quick shower and climbed into his bed. She would have preferred to go home, but after a couple of beers she knew better than to drive and a taxi home tonight and back again in the morning to collect her car just seemed like such a waste of money. Twenty minutes later, she was still awake, and debating the merits of the choice put before her.

What girl wouldn't want three men vying for her attention? At least, that's what she used to think. Now that it was a reality, she didn't know if she should be thrilled or wary. Frankly she was scared to death of having to make a choice between the three friends. Each man had a body that spoke to Tessa's in an earthy and primal way. But more than that, there was a deeper attraction to each of them, something that spoke to her mind and her heart.

But she had thought her ex had spoken to her heart too. She had been so certain of their relationship, so sure they were meant to be together. Could she be wrong again? Could she trust her heart and her mind to know what was really going on? She had been so blind with Rick, and had refused to see his lies until the bitter end. She never wanted to feel like that again.

Was what she felt for these three men the same? Was she being blind again? It didn't feel that way, but how could she trust herself? It just didn't seem possible that the universe would send her three great guys all at once, especially since they were so different from each other.

It seemed that she had always loved Rob, even back in high school. Until recently, it had been the love of friends. Now, she recognized that over time it had developed into something deeper and more intimate. He was her friend, but he might be her soul-mate.

With Peter, she had shared one night of physical bliss, but they had talked for hours, sharing opinions, arguing lightly when they didn't agree. He had a quick wit and intelligence that drew her, that made her want to know him better.

Mitch was the enigma. Sure, the physical attraction was there, but Tessa was an adult and could dismiss and ignore it. Couldn't she? But his blunt candor had an undeniable appeal, as did his playful attitude and friendly ways.

Tessa could easily understand how these three men became close friends since moving into the same neighborhood. It was strange that she hadn't met Rob's friends before, but he often only had a few short days at home when he was on leave, and didn't share his time with Tessa with anyone else. Long ago Rob had told her that because he was deployed overseas, the military forbade him the use any social media. Facebook, Twitter, all of the social media sites were off limits. His commander dictated that the enemy would not be given an easy way to go after his unit or their friends and family. It made his absences seem longer with only the occasional phone call to break the monotony. So, when those rare opportunities to be together arrived, they spent their time with each other and no one else.

Her thoughts flipped back and forth between the three men. It mystified her that they were all so accepting of the competition to win her affection. It was beyond belief, and in her mind, just plain weird. How could they agree to let her see all of them? Not that their agreement was real. It was more of a standoff than anything else. And really it wasn't like they had a choice in who she decided to see. She was a grown woman, and nobody would dictate who she could or would spend time with.

Tessa tried to look at it from the perspectives of Mitch, Peter, and Rob, but couldn't manage it. She just could not wrap her head around the idea of a happy, functional relationship with more than two people. There was no way she would want to share her man with another woman; her selfish ex had taught her that. Until she found out he was dating someone else, she hadn't been the jealous type, but now? Now she was definitely jealous shrew material. How could men agree to share a woman? It didn't make sense, were all men insane?

What the hell was she going to do? How the hell could she possibly choose between them?

"Think about each one separately," she told herself. "What attracts you to them?" She twisted restlessly under the sheet, trying in vain to get comfortable. "How the hell did this happen to me?" She swore graphically, punching the pillow with each word in emphasis. Unbidden an image of the three of them sitting side by side in the hot tub popped into her mind. The image made her breathless. They were all attractive, but so different from one another.

Rob's blonde hair was styled in a military brush cut, deep blue eyes and he was the shortest of the trio at five nine, but he was strong and muscular. Both Mitch and Peter topped six feet. Peter had golden brown eyes and dark brown hair curling at his collar, but still neatly trimmed. He had a muscular but lean runner's body. Mitch had short cropped black hair, bedroom eyes like melted chocolate, broad shoulders, a narrow waist and the sexiest feet she had ever seen.

They were a totally likable and lickable group, that much was certain. How was a girl supposed to resist their charms?

Peter had been such a giving and demanding lover. Driving her to the edge and easing off, pushing and teasing, driving her crazy with a subtle touch, demanding she participate fully to bring them both pleasure.

Rob was a gentle, slow and easy lover, paying detailed attention to each and every inch of her body.

She wondered what making love to Mitch would be like. Would it be slow and gentle? Hard and fast? Maybe a bit kinky? Tessa smiled at that thought. Kinky with Mitch might be fun; she had never done anything kinky.

Of course, before Peter, she had never had sex in a parking lot either. But that night in the parking lot had been electric.

Her fingers idly twirled a strand of hair, then stroked down her cheek, along her neck and across the lace edge of her teddy. Tessa's skin heated at the touch and she sighed softly. Her mind drifted back to the parking lot. She could almost feel Peter's long thin fingers caressing and teasing, plucking at her pebbled nipples. She flipped the sheet back and imagined kissing him while his hands were busy on her body. As her mind provided the images, Tessa's hands provided the reality of touch; stroking and teasing her sensitive breasts.

"Wow, I hope this display means you're thinking about me." Rob's voice startled Tessa out of her fantasy and she jerked her hands away.

"Rob," she exclaimed in surprise. "I didn't expect you back so soon."

"So, this lovely display wasn't meant for me then." He mocked a pout. "Too bad, because it was definitely moving me." He stroked a palm across the bulge in his shorts.

Tessa's blush faded and she beckoned him closer. "Come here, Soldier. Let me check out that weapon you're packing." She bit her lip to hide a grin when he eagerly obeyed her summons.

Tessa woke to the heavenly smell of coffee and the low rumble of a masculine chuckle. She rolled over to cuddle against Rob, only to discover that he was sound asleep. Her sleep-fogged mind wiggled with the conflict. If he was sleeping beside her, who had made coffee, and who was laughing? She clutched the sheet to her chest and bolted upright. More laughter greeted her action. Her gaze flew to the door.

"What the hell are you doing here?" she demanded with a glare.

"Bringing you coffee in bed, Sweetie," Mitch drawled. "How was I to know you were cuddled up with this moron?" He gestured toward Rob with the cup in his hand.

"Maybe because she's in my house and in my bed," Rob growled. "Get out of here Waters." Rob pulled Tessa back down into his embrace. "We are not ready to get up yet. Lock the door on your way out."

Tessa looked back and forth between the two men. It was early, and her mind wasn't up to processing things yet. "Give me that coffee before you leave," she growled at the man lounging indolently against the door jam.

"You want it? Come and get it." He winked at her. "I came over here; made you coffee. The cinnamon buns are in the oven. The least you can do," he winked at her, "is get your butt out of bed and share them with me." He pivoted his head to look at his long-time friend. "Let the lady up, it's just plain wrong to hold her hostage in your bed."

"He is not holding me hostage." Tessa glared at Mitch. "Now give me the coffee and nobody gets hurt."

"Get...the...fuck...out of my bedroom-" Rob roared. "Leave us alone."

Tessa and Mitch both stared at Rob's uncharacteristic outburst.

"Rob," Tessa chided. "You said the f-word. You never say the f-word. Hell, I've known you since grade six. Not once, in all that time, have I ever heard you use the f-word. Holy hell."

She turned to look at Mitch. "You'd better leave; I've never seen him lose his temper. *Ever.*"

Rob struggled to sit up without dropping the sheet to expose Tessa. "I said get the fuck out of my bedroom." He threw a pillow at Mitch. The throw was wildly off, sending Mitch into gales of laughter.

"Okay," Mitch conceded, "I'll leave the bedroom, but I'm not leaving the house." He cocked his head, listening to something. "Oops, there's my dinger. Breakfast is ready." He grinned raunchily at them. "Get your lazy butts out of bed and down to the kitchen." Turning on his heel, he left.

"Bring back that cof-" Rob's hand clamped over Tessa's mouth, stopping her words.

"Don't," he warned her. "Don't say anything to bring him back or we'll never get rid of him." Rob flopped back onto the bed with a sigh. Pulling Tessa into his arms, he snuggled close.

"Darn. I was hoping for a long slow morning in bed with you." He kissed her lightly on the forehead.

Tessa snuggled into his embrace. He was nice and warm and cozy and the morning air was cool. She sighed softly. "Me too." They shared a long lingering kiss, before Tessa pulled away reluctantly. "Damn. I have to pee." She started to wiggle out of bed.

"No way." Rob started tickling her, running his fingers up and down her side, searching out all of the sensitive zones he had found the day before.

Tessa squealed. "Let me go. I ... have ... to ... pee." She writhed under his touch. "Rob. Stop it." She bucked against him.

"Pay the toll," he demanded, his fingers digging lightly into her underarm.

"Yes." She squealed again. "Anything, just let me go."

"Then kiss me like you mean it." His fingers stilled and he drew her back into his embrace.

Tessa rolled onto her back, her arms going around Rob's shoulders, pulling him on top of her. "Anything," she whispered, raising her lips to his.

"You, Tessa Dupree, are mine," he whispered against her mouth. "Don't you ever forget it!" He pressed his lips against hers, softly at first, then increased the pressure and intensity.

Rob's tongue slipped inside Tessa's mouth and she knew he was claiming her with his kiss, as well as his words. She poured her heart into the kiss, telling him without words that she cared for him too. For a moment, her mind battled her heart. Did she love him? Was she prepared to commit to only one man? Was Rob her soul mate? Then the love and power in his kiss, in his caress overpowered all thought and she gave into the sensation, gave in to his love. At length, Rob backed off, and Tessa knew a moment of loss.

"Come on, Sweetie." Rob groaned. "As much as I don't want to give to in my idiot friend, it is time to get up. He won't leave until we show up downstairs. I'm surprised he's not back up here already."

Tessa scampered out of bed and raced into the en-suite. "Your idiot friend keeps interfering in my sex-life," she called out over her shoulder as she closed the door.

"What does that mean?" Rob called through the door.

"Shit." Tessa whispered to herself. "I so should not have said that. What if he finds out about what happened in the parking lot with Peter?" How the hell would she explain that? It was bad enough that Rob knew she was attracted to Peter and had sort-of dated him. He sure didn't need to know that she had screwed him in the parking lot the night they met, or that Mitch had caught them in the act. When would she learn to keep her big mouth shut?

Tessa finished up in the washroom with a shower and tooth brushing. Grabbing Rob's bathrobe off the door she slipped into it and returned to the bedroom. She was surprised to discover that Rob had already headed downstairs. Heaving a big sigh of relief, she slipped into some clothes and followed him to the kitchen.

Katie O'Connor

Chapter Nine

"So, what are we going to do today?" Mitch asked an hour later.

"We?" Tessa asked, with a quirk of her eyebrow.

"We," Mitch affirmed. "You and I. Now that Rob is gone for the day. You and I are going to get to know each other better."

Resentment pooled in her belly. "And if I object to that course of action? If I have other plans?" She sipped her coffee and set the mug down carefully. It wasn't that she had any other plans, but she didn't like him assuming she had nothing better to do than spend time with him. He was a great guy and as sexy as hell in his jeans and t-shirt, but he was a touch more aggressive than she was used to.

"Do you have other plans?"

"That's beside the point. You assume that I have nothing better to do than spend the day with you while Rob is with his folks." Her brow scrunched up. "I don't think I'm okay with you making assumptions about my time and my life."

Mitch studied her for a moment. "I guess I can accept that." He smiled softly. "I would love to spend some time with you today, if you don't have any other plans." He gave her a jaunty wink.

Tessa sighed inwardly. Why was she so unable to resist this man's charms? What was it about him that spoke to her? "Well, I don't have anything planned. So maybe, just maybe, I can spare you a bit of time

109

today." She winked back at him. "What are you thinking we should do?"

♥♥♥

Tessa inhaled deeply, breathing in the scent of the pine trees surrounding them, and the fresh mountain air. They had driven out into the mountains outside the city, and parked the car in a deserted lot. Few people were hiking the remote area during the work week. They spent a few minutes enjoying the small lake before heading up into the hills. She stood beside the car and stared up the hiking trail. "You know that it has been ages since I went hiking, don't you?" She gave Mitch a quizzical look. "Are you sure this is a beginner trail? It looks awful steep."

"Definitely a beginner hike. I wouldn't take someone who is out of shape on an advanced hike. What do you think I am?"

"Out of shape?" she squeaked. "I'll have you know that I am not out of shape. I do kick boxing a couple times every week. I even jog every now and then." She gave him a mock glare and checked the laces on her runners. "I do wish I had hiking boots like yours, rather than just runners."

"Okay, out of shape might have been the wrong phrase." He grinned unrepentantly at her. "How about unaccustomed to hiking?" When Tessa just snorted, he added, "I'll make you a deal. If you like hiking, I'll help you buy a pair of hiking boots."

They shook hands. "Deal," she agreed. She loved being outdoors and hiking with an attractive man would be a fun way to pass the time. Mitch handed her a small backpack and she slipped it on. "What's in the packs?"

"Sun screen, water, lunch, and stuff." He grinned at her. "Clip this onto your pack. Water for the journey." He handed her a small canteen and slipped into a larger backpack and snapped it securely around his waist. "All set?"

Tessa looked up the trail and around the nearly deserted parking area before looking back at Mitch. "I guess so." For a moment, she wondered if it was wise to head into the mountains a man she hardly knew. After a moment of thought, she decided to trust him. Peter seemed to trust him, not that she really knew Peter well either. But Rob trusted him, he had told her so, and he knew they were spending the day together. She decided to accept Mitch based on Rob's trust. Besides, three years of kick-boxing must have taught her something about self-defence.

She shifted the pack to settle it more comfortably. "Let's get this over with."

"Get it over with?" he asked, laughing. "This is supposed to be fun. You sound like you're on the way to an execution. This is a nice walk in the mountains, nature, birds, trees, animals, sunshine. Doesn't any of this move you? Don't you find it inspiring?"

They started up the path. "Okay, I admit I'm being churlish." She laughed. "I just know I'm going to hurt at the end of the day and I'm not looking forward to it. Promise me a soak in your hot tub later?"

"Absolutely, my lovely princess."

"Princess?" Tessa squawked, pretending indignation and bumping his shoulder with hers. "I am not a princess."

"Yes, your highness," he teased shoulder bumping her back with a grin.

She gave him a mock glare before she tilted her head up and nearly stumbled as she enjoyed the feel of the sun on her face. "Oh, this is so lovely." She inhaled deeply. "Smell that fresh air. No smog, just fresh air and pine trees. And sun." They walked in silence for a few minutes, enjoying the solitude. "Why did you ask if it inspired me, earlier? It definitely relaxes me and helps me unwind, but inspire, I don't know about that. Does it inspire you?"

"It does inspire me. I sketch a little and my favorite subjects are kids and nature. I find peace and inspiration up here."

He shrugged dismissively, as if his drawings were unimportant, but Tessa sensed that it was a big part of his life.

"Can I see your drawings sometime?" She asked.

"Shouldn't it be me asking you to come up and see my 'etchings'?" He laughed. "But yeah," he shrugged again, "you can see them whenever you want."

"Why do you do that?" she asked, skirting sideways around a boulder in the pathway.

"Do what?"

"Dismiss your drawing. You make it sound almost...unimportant to you." She peered at him over top of her sunglasses.

"I don't show them around much, they're kind of private. They aren't really any good but I do enjoy the process, it helps me unwind. And think."

"I would love to be able to draw. I'm hopeless at it. I can't draw a straight line with a ruler. I envy anyone who can draw. I don't have a creative bone in my body."

"Everyone does. You just haven't found yours yet. You did put sunscreen on before we left, didn't you?" He asked.

"Quit trying to change the subject, but yeah, I did put on sunscreen. Did you?" When he nodded, she continued. "So, where do you draw?"

"Wherever I feel the urge, I guess. Mostly at home." They rounded a corner in the pathway and entered a wide meadow. "Sh," he whispered. "Look." He pointed across the meadow to where a white-tail deer grazed with her two fawns.

"They're lovely," she whispered back, slightly awestruck, standing motionless to keep from disturbing them. The doe lifted her head and sniffed the air and looked right at them for a long minute before lowering her head to graze again.

Mitch slipped his backpack off and slowly unzipped the outside pocket to extract a pencil and sketchbook. He moved slowly to sit on a large rock fifty feet to their left. With his sketchbook propped on one knee and held steady with his left hand he started drawing with quick, easy motions. Tessa stole up behind him and watched him draw.

Her attention was split between the deer and Mitch's sketchpad. It was fascinating to watch him bring the scene to life with a few strokes of a pencil. He scratched down a rough outline and when the deer continued to graze undisturbed, he began filling in the picture. She stood behind him without moving until her feet began to ache and her mouth went dry from thirst. Soundlessly she opened her canteen and took a deep drink before moving it into his field of vision. He took a drink and with a nod of thanks handed it back and resumed drawing.

She clipped it back onto her pack and pulled her small camera out. Thankful that she had it set to operate soundlessly, she snapped off a few quick pictures of the deer and then a few from different angles of Mitch working. The doe grazed her way toward the trees and suddenly bounded into them, followed closely by the fawns.

"Wow," Tessa sighed. "That was incredible. Let me see your sketch."

Mitch handed her his sketchpad and rose to his feet and stretched.

"This is fabulous." She looked up at him. "I thought you said they weren't any good? Are you insane? This is beautiful." She stared down at the sketch pad. "It's like a black and white photograph. It's almost too real to be a drawing. You could sell this."

"Thanks," he responded humbly and took the book back and stowed it away in his pack. "Shall we go." He waved toward the path.

Tessa looked at him for a minute. It was obvious that he was changing the subject again, and was uncomfortable with her praise. She pursed her lips thoughtfully. So, Mr. Bold and Outspoken had a weak spot. Interesting. Very interesting. "Okay then, let's go. But this discussion isn't finished." She stuck her tongue out at him and headed out the way he gestured.

"Oh my God, I must have been insane to agree to this-!" Tessa growled, sitting down on a boulder and massaging her calves. She slipped her pack off her back and dropped it beside the boulder. "Who wants to spend their day off hiking in the mountains?"

Mitch kneeled in front of her and took her leg in his hands. Massaging gently, he grinned up at her. "You are having a riot and you know it."

"Oh man, that feels so good." She nodded toward where his hands massaged her calf. "You have magic hands." She sighed and leaned back on the flat surface of the rock. "And the sun feels so good. Except for the aching calves, I think I'm in heaven."

The climb hadn't been difficult, but they had hiked for nearly two hours, their progress slow and methodical and allowing plenty of time to enjoy their surroundings and watch the wildlife. A couple times they had stopped to take pictures, or for Mitch to make a quick sketch.

They had talked the whole way, their conversation ebbing and flowing as they progressed up the hillside. They shared stories about work, their childhoods. Their companionship was easy and relaxed and the few silences that fell between them had been comfortable.

Mitch continued to massage her calf and Tessa's eyes drifted shut.

"It is peaceful out here. I find it so relaxing to walk and hike out here on my days off. A lot of the guys on the force play hockey, even in summer, but I suck at skating." He laughed at himself. "Hiking keeps me fit and I ski a bit in the winter." He shifted his hands to her other calf and began slowly stroking the tension out of it.

The slow motions of his hands relaxed her calf and she sighed in bliss. "That feels so good. Thanks." His motions turned from deep massage to something more relaxing and sensual. Just as she started to think that he was going to try and seduce her, his hands stilled and dropped from her leg.

He slipped his backpack off and opened it. "Lunch time," he decreed. Spreading a soft, light blanket over the mossy ground he began extracting containers from the pack and opening them. "Up you get," he chided her. "You have the drinks."

"Mm, do I have to?" She stretched out in the sun, her t-shirt riding up to expose her belly above her shorts. "The sun feels so good," she purred.

"Lunch first, sunbathing later. Grab the box from your pack please."

"Scrooge," Tessa grumbled but slid off the boulder and settled herself on the blanket. She slipped off her shoes and socks before she unzipped the pack and extracted a box of hard, thick cardboard about the size of a shoe box. She flipped the elastics off it and opened to lid to discover two single serving bottles of wine and two glasses. "How come I got the heavy pack?"

"You had the light pack. I've got lunch, water, a first aid kit, and some other stuff." He winked at her. "I'm a man; I wouldn't make you carry the heavy stuff."

She smiled at his thoughtfulness. "Shall I pour?" she asked gesturing toward the wine.

"Nope. First, we have some water. We need to stay hydrated." He passed her a bottle of water with a chunk of ice floating in it. "Drink up." His words were an order, his voice firm and commanding.

Tessa gave him a puzzled look. Where had that dominant tone come from? She wondered about it for a moment and discarded it. She took several long swallows from the bottle before turning her attention to the food Mitch had spread out.

There was a crusty baguette he had broken into manageable chunks, a couple of types of sliced cheese, orange slices, strawberries, and a small container of chocolates. Tessa reached for a chocolate, but Mitch slapped her fingers lightly and told her that chocolate was dessert, not lunch and she had to wait. Feigning a pout, she obeyed.

Mitch fixed her a small plate of food and handed it to her along with a napkin. They ate in silence for a few moments, resting and refuelling. Hunger sated, Tessa stretched out on the blanket and stared longingly at the chocolate. She wasn't really hungry, but she did have a thing for chocolate. At length, Mitch spoke. "Do you want to play a game?" he asked his voice low and seductive.

"What kind of game?" Tessa opened one eye and peeked at him from where she lay on her back soaking up the sun and listening to the breeze in the trees.

"A game of trust."

"Trust?" She echoed, on the verge of sleep.

"Do you trust me?" he asked softly.

"I came to the back end of no-where with you didn't I?"

"That doesn't answer the question. Do you trust me?" His voice compelled an answer.

Tessa thought a long while before answering. Somehow, she knew this was not an idle question, the answer was important to Mitch, to this game he proposed. Did she trust him? She certainly was attracted to him, but trust was a whole different ball of wax. Mitch certainly didn't make her uncomfortable, except for his tendency to state things without clutter or padding. He had never given her that icky feeling of unease that some men could give her. Plus, even if she hadn't met Mitch until recently, he was one of Rob's friends. Rob often talked about Mitch and trusted him. Was that enough?

"I understand if you don't," he advised. "We've only just met. If you don't feel comfortable giving me your full trust, it isn't a problem. We'll just skip the game and finish our hike."

There was no pressure in his voice, no coercion. Tessa got a sense of simple honest inquiry. She rolled on her side and studied him for a moment. He didn't flinch under her gaze, instead he met it unblinkingly.

"Yes," she answered after more thought. "I trust you." She took a moment to savor the warm smile that spread across his face and lit his melted chocolate eyes, and then rolled back onto her back to soak up more sun. "So, tell me about this game. How does trust fit into it?"

"It's a bit like truth or dare," he replied. "Only I get to direct everything, and you just play along."

Tessa wasn't sure his answer made sense, but for the moment she would play along. "Go ahead then," she said by way of agreement. She stretched and rolled her shoulders, the sun felt so good, just warm enough to be comfortable, but with enough of a breeze to keep cool. She lifted the hem of her T-shirt and exposed her abdomen to the sun's warming rays.

"Why don't you take that off? We're alone out here, off the beaten path. Nobody will see you." Tessa popped open one eye in a questioning glance. "Uh uh, no peeking. That's rule number one. Keep your eyes closed unless I tell you otherwise." He waggled one finger at her. Obediently she closed her eyes. "Take your shirt off," Mitch's voice held a hint of command. "You're wearing a bra, it's as much coverage as that skimpy swimsuit you had on yesterday, and the sun will feel good on your skin." His voice was low and seductive, but still managed to convey the idea as a command rather than a suggestion.

She smiled to herself. That's what he thinks; this was the sexiest bra she owned. Tessa wiggled out of her T-shirt. Bunching it up, she used it as a pillow. She bit back another grin at the sound of Mitch's harsh intake of breath.

"Jesus," he whispered reverently. "I wasn't expecting hot pink lace and black ribbon. Mother of God, don't women wear plain old cotton anymore?"

Tessa laughed and stroked on finger idly along the lace edge of the bra, down into the valley of her cleavage. "I haven't worn white cotton since I had my first job. I spent my entire first paycheck on lingerie. I think maybe I'm addicted." Her finger traced the edge of the bra up the other breast. Her nipples pearled from the light tough. There was something so sensual, so erotic about lying partially clothed in the sun, showing off her body to this attractive, sexy man.

"Question, how do you stay fit?"

Mitch's abrupt change of subject threw her off for a moment. "Muay Tai, kick boxing three times a week and some jogging. Why?"

"Curious. Part of the game. You have a beautiful body."

Tessa's face colored at the compliment, and she barely resisted the urge to disagree. "Thank you," she murmured softly.

"You're welcome. Why kick-boxing?"

"Rob recommended it. But it isn't the cardio-kickboxing that you see on TV. This is the real thing, for self-defence. Just in case." She really didn't want to get into all the sordid details.

"I got that when you said Muay Tai. In case of what?" When she didn't answer right away he added, "You don't have to tell me."

"Three years ago, I was attacked on my way home from a club. I wasn't hurt, just scared. Some bastard was trying to rape me. I got lucky." She sighed. "I smashed him upside the head with my purse. It had a heavy hardcover book in it." She laughed. "Good thing I didn't go home after class and went straight to the bar."

"That's brutal. Some bastards don't deserve to live. Did they catch him?" Mitch's voice was low and tight with suppressed anger.

"Caught and convicted. I knocked him out cold. But I was scared for a long time. Very scared. I didn't want to leave the house. That's when Rob suggested the kickboxing classes. I'm glad he did. Now I'm fit and strong and not helpless."

Mitch laughed. "It doesn't sound like you were helpless anyway. But I'm glad you weren't hurt, and that you can defend yourself."

Abruptly, Mitch asked another question. "What's your favorite color? Mine is navy. Of course, that hot pink bra might just entice me to change my mind."

"Green, I think. Maybe blue. I guess it depends on the day." She wondered for a moment where this was all heading. Mitch proceeded to ask a series of innocuous questions one after another, his pace slow and easy, unhurried. Tessa heard him rustle around in his pack and something cool and hard was put into her hand.

"Sunscreen. We don't want all the luscious skin to burn. Put it on, or do you want me to do it?" There was a hint of challenge in his voice, almost as if he was daring her to let him touch her.

What the hell. Come get me, Mitch. "You do it. I'm too lazy to move." The air was dead still for a moment, the only sound the distant buzzing if flies and a hint of wind in the trees. Then Mitch shifted almost soundlessly and took the bottle from her hand. The top snicked open and the cream spurted out into his hand. A spicy scent wafted to Tessa and the sound of his hands rubbing together reached Tessa's ears seconds before she felt his hands on her stomach.

"Oh, you warmed it." She almost purred at the soft feel of his slippery hands stroking her belly. His hands moved softly, but briskly, spreading the sun screen over her abdomen, up her arms to her shoulders and finally down onto the exposed tops of her breasts. His touch was a strange combination of sensual and impersonal. Tessa was disappointed, she had hoped for more.

"What is your favorite sexual position?" he asked bluntly, his hands leaving her body. "Tessa?" He prompted when she didn't immediately respond.

"I'm thinking." She scrunched up her nose. "I don't think I actually have a favorite. But I haven't had doggy-style for a long time. I think that could move me today." Just the idea of kneeling before Mitch, waiting for him, knowing he would be ogling her ass was enough to arouse Tessa. She squirmed on the blanket, wishing he would suggest it, wishing he would initiate something.

"Take off your shorts," Mitch demanded, completely ignoring Tessa's confession.

"What?" The query exploded from her mouth without thought.

"Trust. Remember?"

Arousal shot up Tessa's spine. Did she want to do this? Did she want to expose herself more fully to Mitch? Their relationship was new and they hadn't really found a direction yet. Hell, she didn't even know if they had a relationship! The command in his voice was soft, but it affected her strongly. Her fingers fumbled with the button on her denim shorts and she slipped them off with almost no hesitation.

"Very good," he praised in unison with the sound of the sunscreen opening. Slowly, Mitch massaged sunscreen onto her legs, his motions going from slow and methodical to slow and sensual. "You have lovely skin." His fingers lingered at the edge of her pink and black lace panties. "And I am definitely developing a fondness for pink."

One hand on each leg, Mitch stroked her legs with long slow strokes from ankle the upper thigh. His fingers traced the edge of her panties, slowly slipping toward her core. Surprised, Tessa snapped her legs shut.

"Uh uh," he chided. "Open up for me. Trust me Tessa. I won't hurt you."

Her limits felt pushed, like he was asking too much. Wasn't it enough that she was laying before him virtually naked? Did he need to see more? Did she want him to know that her panties were damp with arousal? She was so aroused already, simply from exposing herself to his gaze and following his commands. A rush of embarrassment washed over her, and helpless to resist him she relaxed her legs.

"Good girl." He stroked her inner thighs softly. "Wider. Open all the way for me." He gave her a light smack on the inside of her left thigh, urging her to obey.

Biting her lip to keep from groaning, Tessa obeyed, praying he wouldn't notice the moisture staining her underwear. But her prayers were in vain.

"What's this?" he asked, stroking one finger across the moist patch on her panties. "Are you aroused? Do you like this game?" When she didn't answer he growled low in his throat. "Answer me Tessa. Are you hot? Does your pussy need attention?" He stroked one finger slowly up and down her cleft.

She bit her lip again, holding in a groan. Embarrassment battled arousal for control and she flushed deeply, not sure which one triumphed. She grunted her agreement.

"Words Tessa," he demanded, his thumb moving in small circles over her clit. "Tell me in words or I'll stop." His thumb fell motionless for a second.

"Yes," she grunted. When his motions stilled again, she clarified her response. "Yes. It feels good. I need it. Don't stop."

He rewarded her by laying down beside her, one hand nestled between her thighs, the other sliding under her head and pulling her close. Her right arm was under him, he lay there, propped up on his elbow, looking down at her for several long moments and Tessa was tempted to open her eyes, or to speak and break the silence. Squirming against the heat of his gaze, she bit her lip and hoped he would get on with it. A shadow blocked the sun and her eyes flew open.

Her worried gaze met his calm reassuring one. "Close your eyes," he whispered, lowering his mouth and capturing hers in a deep soul stealing kiss.

His mouth tasted of wine and oranges with a hint of something masculine underneath; it sent a wave of arousal coursing through her. Her hips writhed, searching, her toes curled and her nipples pebbled harder. His tongue traced her lips and she groaned low, opened her mouth, granting him access. Their tongues battled for a moment before he pulled away.

Mitch's hand traced up across her belly, cupped her breast lightly and trailed down her arm. Grasping her hand in his, he pulled it up, alongside his shoulder and imprisoned it in his other hand. She stiffened beside him, braced to fight and run if she needed too. Briefly her mind flittered to her ex. He had always liked to be in control; of their lovemaking and of her life. Did she want that again? She wasn't sure.

"Shh," he purred in her ear. His tongue flicked her earlobe. "Anytime you want me to let go, or stop all you have to do is ask."

Was he telling the truth? Unease warred with arousal. Think dammit, she chided herself mentally. What the hell have you gotten yourself into? Why the hell had she agreed to go hiking with this man? Why had she agreed to his game?

In an instant she knew why. She was attracted to him, she had been from the moment she met him. Rob and Peter trusted him. Was that enough for her? "Stop!" she demanded in a low, firm voice.

Mitch released her hand and sat up instantly.

"Do you swear to stop if I ask?" She rolled toward him, propped herself on one elbow and looked at him, hoping she would be able to read his face.

He placed a hand over his heart. "I swear. I won't do anything you don't want. One word and I'll stop. I swear on my badge." He met her gaze unflinchingly. "We can head home now if you want to…"

She studied him, pondering his proposal and her situation. Logic kicked in. Rob and Peter trusted him and knew she was with him.

Tessa smiled and flopped back on her back. "What the hell," she declared. "Do your worst." She grabbed him by the back of the head and pulled his mouth to hers. "Kiss me, Mitch. Kiss me hard."

He pulled back and looked at her with one eyebrow quirked. "You do realize that I give the orders here?" He gave her a roguish grin. "And if you don't obey, you pay a forfeit."

Her mouth opened in a silent 'oh' and his mouth crushed against it, his tongue delving deep. Before Tessa realized what was happening, he had both her arms pinned above her head. Mitch reached behind him, clearly searching for something. "Back to the game," he declared, his hands busy binding hers with a length of soft silk. He looked down at Tessa, studying her from head to toe and back again, his gaze lingering on her face, her bound wrists still trapped in his hands.

"Okay?" he asked.

Tessa writhed a bit against the bonds, and smiled up at him. "Okay." She puffed out a breath, revelling in the hint of fear and uncertainty her precarious position caused.

"Good. Now, if I release your hands, do you promise to hold them still?" At her nod, he let go of her silk-bound hands and pivoted to straddle her waist. Kneeling above her he looked down, and grinned. "Babe, you look so sexy there, all tied up, my hostage. And I am going to tease you like you have never been teased before." He waited for a response. She writhed under him, her body speaking for her.

"Close those eyes." Tessa obeyed without complaint. "Now, rule number two, no speaking unless I ask you a question." Tessa nodded her compliance. "Very good."

Mitch traced the line of her bra, one finger sliding down each side toward the center. "I love your breasts." He flicked the center clasp open, his hands cupping her breasts, holding the thin covering in place. He bent low, his tongue tracing the path his fingers had just taken; down one side, across the valley in between her beasts, up the other side to nibble her ear and back again. His thumbs traced slow teasing circles on her nipples and Tessa writhed under his touch, moaning low in her throat.

He paused a moment, testing her, seeing if she would speak. He rewarded her silence by flicking the bra off her breasts, exposing them to the air and his mouth. He bathed one nipple, then the other with his tongue before sucking the left deep into his mouth and nibbling on it lightly. Tessa arched under his caress, shivers of delight ricocheting through her, lodging at the juncture of her thighs. The pleasure was so intense, the throbbing so strong that she feared she might orgasm from this alone. Her breath came in short staccato bursts, harsh and erratic.

"Do you like that, Sweetheart?" Mitch teased around a mouthful of nipple, his fingers toying with the other nipple.

"Yes. Oh god, yes." Tessa cried, aching against him, bucking her hips in search of release. She started to reach for him, but at the last second recalled her promise to keep her hands above her head and dropped them back with a whimper. The sensations were overwhelming. The heat of the sun, the feel of Mitch's hands and mouth on her skin, his soft murmurs of approval, the feeling of being helpless. Tessa felt her pussy gush, its soft folds growing moist with her arousal.

Mitch shifted to the side, moving off Tessa, his hands never halting their delightful assault. He trailed kisses down her abdomen, lingering and tasting along the line of her panties. With a brisk motion of his hand her panties were down and off. The warm air felt startlingly good on the heated flesh of her pussy and she spread her legs, loving the sensation of sun and air on her moist lips. Then, all thoughts fled.

Mitch's hands and mouth were everywhere. Touching, tasting, teasing, and driving Tessa wild with desire, sending shockwaves of arousal coursing through her. His fingers tested her moisture, and he breathed his approval finding her wet and ready. One finger slid inside then another, pumping her slowly, his palm rubbing against her clit, driving Tessa closer and closer to orgasm and backing off before she peaked. His mouth played homage to her breasts, making her writhe and twitch under his assault.

"What do you want, Tessa?" He whispered in her ear.

"You," she gasped. "I need you inside me."

His laughter tickled her neck. He rolled away from Tessa, and made quick work of removing his clothing. Tessa heard the crinkle of foil and knew without looking that he was donning protection.

"Hurry," she begged before realizing her mistake. "Shit," she whispered and then groaned at the additional failure to remain silent.

"Tsk. Tsk." Mitch chided her. "Time to pay for your transgressions." He sounded almost gleeful. "Roll onto your stomach." His voice brooked no argument and Tessa obeyed immediately.

"On your knees and elbows," he commanded with a slap on her ass for emphasis.

Tessa obeyed and froze in place. Her mind and body were whirling. She was awash in sensation and emotion. She was aroused, nervous, excited, confused, obedient and defiant all at once. Part of her screamed to bolt, to stop the game, but a bigger part of her demanded she stay still, and take what was coming to her. What would the forfeit for disobedience, for speaking be? She posed there obedient, nervous and excited.

Mitch moved to kneel behind her. His fingers traced the line of her spine and he splayed his hands across the breadth of her ass. Touching, exploring and teasing. "Don't move," he commanded and she felt something touch her pussy lips. "If you move one muscle, if you so much as twitch in place, I'll stop." He warned.

With a small thrust of his hips, he entered her. The tip of his cock slid into her slick opening. Tessa sucked in a breath at the sudden motion, but didn't move. After a moment, Mitch moved again, slowly pulling away and then sliding back in; each stroke longer and deeper than the last until after numerous agonizing strokes he was seated fully inside her core. He knelt behind her, motionless, his cock buried to the hilt, his balls resting against Tessa's clit.

"God, your ass is beautiful." He groaned, stroking it reverently. He grasped her hips and pumped slowly in and out of her, his pace keeping Tessa on the brink, but too slow to push her over the edge. She wanted to thrust against him, to beg for more, but knew Mitch would stop and leave her hanging there unfulfilled.

His cock glided in and out slowly, teasingly and Tessa felt something nudge against the puckered tightness of her anus. Her entire body tightened up at the unexpected sensation.

"Relax, it's just a finger," Mitch advised, his finger making slow circles around her opening.

Tessa tried to remember to breathe. She drew in a shuddering, shaking breath and forced herself to relax under his assault.

"Relax. Trust me," he murmured and leaned over, digging into his pack once again.

How much stuff does he have in that thing? Tessa wondered before she heard the snap of a flip cap and felt something cool and moist dribble onto her sphincter. Mitch's finger returned to tease her some more, slowly pressing and easing inside her ass. His cock twitched inside her pussy and she clenched in response.

"Stay still," he warned. "No more moving. Not even a twitch. I'll give you that one, but only because it's your first time." He said generously, but pushed his finger deeper into her ass. Slowly he pushed his finger in as he pulled his cock out. Then, he reversed the strokes. One going in as the other came out.

Tessa focused, took several deep breaths and forced herself to relax.

"Relax." He pushed against her with another finger. "Have you ever had anal sex?"

Tessa clenched around him, partly in fear, partly in arousal. "No." She whispered.

"Have you ever wanted to?" he persisted.

"Um."

"Trust Tessa. Trust me with your secrets." His voice was a low purr of seduction.

"Yes," she confessed quietly, wondering what it was about this man that made her want to trust him and made her want to try this taboo thing. "But I've never had the chance." She blushed red, her confession embarrassing her as much at it aroused them both.

"May I teach you?" Mitch asked, his voice holding both a command and uncertainty.

Tessa dropped her head; her long hair hid her face and muffled her voice. "Yes, please," she murmured. Longing raced through her. "What do I . . . we do? Will it fit?" Her voice quivered slightly.

"It will fit," he reassured her. "In all honesty, I'm not a large man." Mitch's left hand traced long sensuous lines down Tessa's spine, while his right continued to play with and tease her tight hole. "It's all about relaxation," he purred behind her, his hands busy. "A bit of lube, relaxation and patience is all it takes."

Tessa sucked in a startled breath and then laughed when Mitch's cock twitched inside her. "Patience, you say?"

"I didn't say patience was easy." He punctuated his words with a few quick thrusts. "We just have to go slow. Now, no more talking. Just relax, feel and enjoy." Stilling the motion of his hips, Mitch eased a second finger past the tight barrier of her ass. Then he eased slowly away from her until his cock popped free and her aching pussy was left empty and bereft.

Tessa made a grunt of enquiry and peered over her shoulder at Mitch, her confusion in her eyes.

"Tessa, Sweetie, you might be willing to try anal, but there is no way that this tight hole, or you are ready for double penetration. We'll teach you that later." He punctuated his words by making small circles with his fingers, toying with her anus, stretching it out.

Something cool dribbled low on her crack and Tessa moaned in shock. More lube. Mitch spread the lube around, added more and worked her looser and looser. Tessa wiggled and squirmed under the erotic, sometimes uncomfortable assault, and all the while Mitch whispered words of encouragement and endearments. At one point, Tessa realized that her fear had vanished, had been replaced by excitement and anticipation.

"Move with me," Mitch encouraged. "Make it feel good for you. Push your hips back." Tessa obeyed, her slight motion causing her to tighten up. "Oops, not like that. Breathe deep, now rock forward and back on your hands and knees. Move your whole body, not just your hips. Slow and steady. That's a girl." He dribbled more lube where his fingers met her body. "Pump yourself onto me."

Tessa focused on relaxing and pushing back her hips. Bit by tiny bit, Mitch's fingers slid deeper and deeper inside her. With each slow rocking motion, he penetrated further. "Oh god," she whispered, "it feels so good."

"That's it love, feel it. Ride it." His hands pumped in opposition to her hip motions. "That's it," he repeated. "I'm pulling out now."

The loss of his fingers left Tessa feeling bereft. Cool lube dribbled down her crack again and she wriggled at the slippery, cool sensation. Then, something hard and warm, and much larger than Mitch's fingers was pressed against her.

Mitch leaned forward to press a kiss on her back. "Slow and easy, Tessa. I'm not going to move. Push back." She wriggled a bit and he sucked in a breath. "Damn, this is killing me," he confessed. "What the hell was I thinking?"

Power flooded through Tessa. Mitch needed her. Needed her badly, yet he was giving her the power to complete this, the control to take him inside her tight ass or to stop if she needed to. What a thrill! Moisture flooded her already wet pussy and a shiver of excitement raced across her skin leaving it tingling and cool in spite of the warm sun. Slowly, she pressed backwards against his cock. She could feel his hand between them, holding it steady.

Somehow, she knew the angle wasn't quite right. Mitch's cock didn't slip right inside her, so she twisted her hips up and bit and then down. There it was, the tip parted her tight ass and she groaned in delight. Mitch said he wasn't well endowed, but his cock was definitely bigger than his fingers. Only the very tip was inside, but she felt stretched and full already. She stopped moving, and took three deep breaths, willing herself to relax, before she pushed back against him once more. His cock was like a hard steel rod pressed against her, entering her. Filling her.

Mitch dropped his hand away from his cock, and grabbed Tessa by both hips. He didn't move, didn't force her to take more, instead he knelt there motionless, twitching with impatience, but willing to let Tessa set the pace.

Tessa pulled forward and pumped backwards again, her motions slow and steady. Each thrust of her hips drew him deeper inside her tight cavern. It hurt, just a bit, but at the same time it felt good. Waves of arousal rushed through her. Her breasts were swollen and sensitive, her nipples diamond hard. She kept pumping, revelling in the feel of his hardness slipping inside her ass as it relaxed on each stroke. Then suddenly, he was inside her, she could feel his belly pressed fully against her bum, his balls bouncing off the wet lips of her pussy and against her throbbing clit.

"Oh geez," Mitch groaned then swore repeatedly. "Come on, girl. You're killing me."

Tessa laughed and started pushing back against him, rocking faster. Harder. "Yes," she groaned loudly, her thrusts getting more frantic. As she pumped harder, his balls slapped against her clit, each tap driving her higher and closer to her peak. "Oh," she groaned. "Please."

"Yes-" Mitch groaned aloud and started pumping against her.

Sensations swamped Tessa, and she became helpless to do anything but react, to pump with Mitch, to drive them closer and closer to the edge. Harder and harder they moved in unison, pleasure building, swamping her, until shards of desire exploded over her, sending her over the edge into a world of exploding sensation. She gave in to the feelings and rode her orgasm out.

When she came back down to reality, Mitch was motionless behind her; his breathing harsh and uneven, his cock twitching and shrinking inside her. She had been so lost in her own pleasure that she was unaware of his release. His hands traced lazy circles on her back. "Oh man," he declared breathlessly, "I think I need a nap." Leaning down he kissed her on the shoulder blade and eased out of her. "Lay down, Tessa. Get off your knees."

Soft hands guided her to the blanket and she sighed in bliss. "That was delicious." She giggled. "Can you call anal sex delicious?"

"You can call it anything you like," Mitch agreed, quickly and efficiently disposing of the condom in a small garbage bag before dropping to the blanket beside Tessa. "I'm going to call it fabulous." He leaned on one elbow and looked down at her, concern darkening his eyes. "I didn't hurt you, did I?" He blushed. "I kind of got carried away. Man, the effect you have on me is unbelievable. I've never been moved like this before."

Tessa rose up on one elbow, grabbed his head and pulled him down for a long, slow kiss. "That was incredible. You didn't hurt me. Well, it might have stung a bit. But I'm fine, more than fine." She flopped back down and groaned. "But I'm not sure I want to do any more hiking." She winked and laughed.

"Fear not, lovely maiden." Mitch handed her a bottle of water. "Well rest up and return to the car. Slowly."

It was some time later before the dressed and headed back down the hill and Tessa asked the question that had been nagging at her subconscious since Mitch pulled out his anal plug.

"Were you so sure of me then? You came prepared for sex, for anal sex?" She was more curious than offended, but still wanted to know.

Mitch pulled her into his embrace and placed a light kiss on the top of her head. "Hell no, just very, very hopeful. You're a beautiful, sensual woman, Tessa. I've wanted to make love to you since stumbling on you and Peter in the parking lot. Getting to know you at my party and today only made that need grow." He shrugged and kissed her again.

"I didn't think for one minute that you were easy," he explained, "just desirable. And I have to confess, that one date with you isn't going to be enough. Not even close." He popped the trunk of his car open and they dropped their packs inside and moved to get into the car.

Mitch slipped his sun-glasses off and studied Tessa over the roof while they waited for the mountain air to circulate through the sun heated car and cool it. "I would like to see you again."

"I think I would like that." Tessa studied Mitch, loving the way the sun glinted in his black hair and made his dark eyes shine. "I enjoyed myself today." She slid into the car, grateful that the seats were plush cloth, not vinyl.

She looked at him and laughed. "Before we leave, fetch those chocolates from the trunk. I've worked up an appetite. And crank up the air conditioning, before I melt."

Katie O'Connor

Chapter Ten

Tessa stumbled up the steps to Rob's front door. Today had been her first hike for years; she had definitely overdone it. Muscles hurt that she hadn't even known she had. Her legs felt like lead.

"Oh man, I really hurt." She grimaced at Mitch. "I may never walk upright again."

Mitch steadied her and reached past her to open the door. "I could have taken you to your place." He reiterated his earlier offer.

"My bag is here, and my car. If you drove me home I would have to walk to work, and I'm not going to be fit to walk for a year at least." She flashed him a cheeky grin and stepped into the house. "Rob, I'm back."

Rob stepped out of the kitchen and wrapped her in his arms. "Good, I was starting to worry."

His arms were strong and gentle around her shoulders. He kissed her gently on the cheek. "Come on in, I'll draw you a bath. Dinner is almost ready." He led her toward the bathroom.

Tessa wiggled out of his grasp and gave him a bit of a glare. Did he think she would just abandon her date at the doorway? She hobbled back to Mitch and kissed him on the cheek. "Thank you. I had a lovely day."

"Can I see you again?" he asked, completely ignoring Rob.

"I think I would like that," Tessa replied honestly, punctuating her words with a quick hug. "Have a good night."

"Good night, beautiful. Rob, take care of this lovely woman." His words were laden with warning. He cast a stern look at his friend, smiled at Tessa and slipped out, pulling the door shut behind him. Tessa stared at the closed door. Why did men have to be so difficult and territorial?

"Let's get you into that tub. A nice soak in Epsom salts will relax those sore muscles." He helped her hobble up the stairs. "You really overdid it."

"Ah," she groaned. "It didn't seem like it at the time. I didn't stiffen up until I tried to get out of the car." She flopped down onto the toilet and rubbed her aching thighs. "Damn I hurt." She flexed her shoulders. "Even my back and shoulders hurt. How can you hurt your shoulders on a hike? I thought I was fairly fit."

Rob laughed. "Kick-boxing and jogging don't work the same muscles as hiking, and if I know Mitch you climbed some steep hills and clambered over a bunch of boulders." Rob sprinkled Epsom salts in the tub and turned the water on. It gushed over his hand as he adjusted the temperature. Satisfied he had it perfect, he poured in a shot of bubble bath and the soft scent of roses filled the room.

"You have bubble bath?" she asked in surprise.

"I picked it up today, for you. I knew you would need a soak." He winked at her. "Let me help you out of those clothes and into the tub. I thought the privacy of a bath might be nicer than soaking in Mitch's hot tub."

Tessa smiled when he knelt before her and untied her shoes before slipping them off. He was gentle and careful as he undressed her, helping her move without rushing her. His tender touches warmed her heart. There was nothing sexual in his actions, just care and attention. He handed her a hair elastic from the drawer and she quickly gathered her curls into a messy pile on top of her head. "Thanks."

She smiled up at him as he held her hand, helping her lower herself into the steaming water.

"Oh god, that feels good." A soft sigh escaped her as she slid deeper into the water.

Rob picked up a fireplace lighter off the counter and lit a trio of chubby candles near the tub's faucet. "You rest a bit," He said, gathering up her clothing. "I need to check on dinner." He slipped out of the room, flipping off the light and leaving the door slightly ajar.

Tub filled, Tessa turned the faucet off, leaned back, closed her eyes and slowed her breathing. Breathe in for four counts, long, slow counts and out for the same. Kick boxing had taught her the value of controlling her breathing to help relax.

Rob knocked softly on the bathroom door and stuck his head around the corner. "I brought you some wine." He slipped into the room and placed a glass of red wine on the edge of the tub.

Before she could muster up the strength to thank him he was gone again. She slipped the wine, enjoying its fruity aftertaste and slightly sweet aroma. She recognized the taste immediately. Even after being on tour for the better part of a year, he had remembered her favorite wine.

♥♥♥

"Let me warm the water up for you." Rob's words slowly penetrated Tessa's sleep-like fog. She pulled her legs up to her chest as he ran a bit of water to be sure it was warm before pulling the plug and partially draining the tub. Warm water splashed into the tub. "Turn it off when you have enough. I'll be back in a few minutes."

When the water was warm enough and deep enough she reached forward and shut off the tap. The bathroom door eased open and Rob strode in carrying a tray. He settled the tray on the edge of the tub and flopped down on the floor.

"Dinner is served."

"In the tub?" she squeaked. "I've never eaten in the tub. "He handed her a bowl and a fork. "Then you are missing something special. Eat your salad." He picked up a bowl and leaned back against the wall to eat. When you are finished your greens, we have barbecue chicken breasts, and baked potatoes."

His words sparked her appetite and she dug into her salad. "Oh, that's good. Is that strawberry?"

"It is my own recipe. Or rather my grandmother's. It is an apple-strawberry cream dressing. Try a bite of the cheddar with it."

"Oh man, that is good. Where did you learn to cook?"

"The army, sort of. I did a couple weeks in the kitchen in one of our camps while I had an injury to my leg. I learned what not to do. Army food sucks. On my next trip home, I had Gramms give me some lessons. She is probably the world's best cook. Nothing fancy, just plain, good food that fills you up.

I've been practising. Wait until you taste my Black Forest cake."

"How come I didn't know that you cooked?"

"Tessa, you've known me for years, but there are a lot of things about me that you don't know. Things you didn't notice."

"I can't believe I didn't know you loved me," she responded to the words he didn't say. "I must have been blind."

"Not blind, distracted. You had your own life." There was no condemnation in his words, just understanding.

"How could you stand being around me when I was so … so oblivious?" She shook her head in confusion.

"Remember Aunt Grace and Uncle Allen?"

It took her a moment to clue into the subject change. When she recalled who he was talking about, Tessa nodded.

Rob continued. "I watched them dance around each other for years. Uncle Allen was Gramms' neighbor and he spent a lot of time at her house. He came to every family gathering. It was years after her divorce before Aunt Grace noticed him." He smiled at the memory. "Even as a kid I noticed what was going on between them, or rather what wasn't going on." He set their salad bowls aside and took the covers off their main courses. He handed her a plate, picked up his own and leaned back again.

"Gramms and I talked about it a lot. It's like the song says … 'you can't hurry love.' Gramms helped me to realize that you might never love me, but that didn't mean I should give up."

"She told you to keep after me even if I didn't love you? Why would she do that?"

"Yes and no. She told me 'Don't give up until Tessa has settled down for good with someone else.' As long as you weren't serious about anyone, there was hope for me. For us. Love finds a way. So, I stuck it out even though you drove me crazy with the fools you dated."

Tessa laughed. "I did date some prizes, didn't I?"

"I don't want to talk about it anymore. It's bad enough I have to share you with Mitch and Peter. I definitely don't want to talk about you and other guys. I lived through that once and I hope I never have to live through it again." He leaned over and kissed her on the cheek. "Finish your dinner; that water has to be getting cold."

"I don't know why you waited for me," she said quietly, after a few minutes of thought.

"That one is easy. You are worth waiting for." He rose to his feet and smiled down at her. "You make me happy. I know guys don't admit to things like this, but just knowing you are in my world pleases me. I might not have liked it, but if being with someone else is what you wanted, needed, then it was all right by me. Even if it hurt. Your happiness means more than mine." He scooped up the tray and left the bathroom, as if he were uncomfortable with his confession.

"Wow," she whispered to his retreating back. Warmth flooded through her. Her heart felt like it would burst with happiness. This was new, this having someone love you so much and make a declaration like that. She felt giddy with excitement and moved to tears all at once.

How many guys had she dated that had been jealous when she talked to another man? All of them it seemed. And now here was Rob putting her happiness above his own. Incredible. She rose from the tub, dried off. She wrapped herself in Rob's bathrobe and headed toward the kitchen to enjoy his company and some of that cake he was bragging about.

Katie O'Connor

Chapter Eleven

"How many times are you going to check your phone today?" Becky stuck her head through the door of Tessa's tiny office and smiled. "Expecting something important?"

"I can't believe how many messages I am getting," Tessa replied with a grimace. "I've lost count at the number of texts. It's a good thing I have a private office. If I waited until I got off work, I would never catch up."

"What's so all fired important? It isn't like you to check messages except on coffee break."

"I checked at break and I had twenty-seven unread texts. I'm just trying to stay on top of them." She sighed heavily. "This has to end."

"Your trio, I assume?" Becky teased.

"God yes," Tessa buried her head in her hands. "I don't know what to do. It's like they can't let a minute go by without contacting me. It's driving me f'ing nuts."

Becky raised an eyebrow at Tessa's near profanity. "Oh?"

"I saw Rob and Mitch yesterday. I woke up to texts from Mitch. I wasn't even out of the shower this morning before I had messages from all of them. I swear they are egging each other on." She huffed out a frustrated breath.

"So, tell them to stop texting." She gave Tessa a stern, motherly look.

Tessa flushed bright red. "I can't. I love it. Even though I hate it, I love it. Does that make any sense?" She dropped her forehead to the desk. When her friend laughed aloud, Tessa lifted her head long enough to glare. "Some help you are."

"What are you going to do?" Becky asked, totally ignoring Tessa's chastisement.

"Rob asked me to go for a walk right after work. Peter and I are having dinner at seven-thirty and Mitch wants to go to a movie later."

"You're going to date them all in one night?" Becky's eyes widened with shock. "Is that a good idea?"

"It's definitely a bad idea. So, I'm putting off Rob and Mitch. I spent the whole day with them yesterday. Peter is bringing over pizza and a DVD. Is it pathetic that I only agreed because it required no effort on my part and I'm starving?"

"Yup."

Tessa gave Becky a squinty-eyed look. "Thanks for the support," she drawled sarcastically. "I'm having trouble coping with this already."

"Honey, you don't have problems. We should all be so cursed to have three guys chasing us. I don't have any." She smiled wanly. "This could turn out to be stressful for you."

"It already is, and it's only been a day and a half." Tessa shook her head. "How do I tell them no? How do I stop myself from wanting to spend time with them all? When did my life get so complicated?" She looked thoughtful for a moment before adding, "I'll take any advice you have to give."

"If you want my opinion, take it slow. Spend time with each of them, alone. But save time for yourself and for your girlfriends. This is going to be a balancing act like you have never attempted before. If you aren't careful, the stress will pull you under. But I'm the last person you should be asking for relationship advice. My love life sucks." Becky frowned briefly before pasting on a smile.

"Ouch. Sorry, I forgot about that. Are you going to call him?" Tessa pushed her chair back, went to the door and embraced her friend sympathetically.

"I can't decide. I think I will … maybe not." Becky shook her head indecisively. "Definitely not. He knows where to find me if he wants to see me again. The man infuriates me."

"It's been a long time since you dated anyone. Maybe it's time."

"Maybe it's not." Her reply was abrupt and snappish. "Anyway, I just stopped to tell you I have a meeting with my supervisor. I'll catch you later. Good luck with your trio." She stepped back, gave a quick wave and disappeared out the door.

"Well she was absolutely no help. Why can't love be easier?" Tessa pondered the difficulties her friend was having for a moment before she turned her attention back to her paperwork. When she heard the chirping of her phone's message indicator, she forced herself to ignore it. She had a boat load of paperwork to finish before she could leave and she was starving; there was no sense in getting distracted.

A persistent pounding assaulted her ears when Tessa shut off the shower and stepped from the tub. She glared at her cell phone when it started vibrating across the bathroom counter. A groan escaped her. "You have got to be kidding. He can't be early."

Snatching it up she glanced at the caller ID. "Damn. Peter. Really?" After a calming breath she answered the call. "Hello?"

His voice sounded just a touch tinny. "Tessa, are you okay? I've been knocking for five minutes."

"I was in the shower. Give me a minute to get dressed."

"Don't get dressed on my account."

His deep chuckle sent shivers down her spine and a smile to her lips. "Nice try," she drawled. "Hold tight and I'll be right there." She ended the call and tossed the phone back on the counter. Damn she hadn't plan on having to hurry. She had been hoping for a few minutes to relax before Peter arrived.

Torn between making him wait and avoiding the gossip of leaving him in the hallway, Tessa threw some clothes on her still damp body, ran a brush through her very damp hair and hurried to let him in.

"Hi." she greeted him breathless from her rush to get dressed.

"Hi yourself," he murmured, cupping her cheek gently and drawing her close for a kiss. "It's so good to see you." He brushed his thumb lightly across her cheek and cupped her neck, drawing her close for another kiss.

The light touch of his thumb across her cheek was like a whisper of air. His hand brushed across her cheek to cup her neck lightly. Light pressure on her neck urged her toward his, she couldn't help but answer his silent beckoning, and she leaned in tilting her head in welcome. A soft moan escaped her before their lips met. The first touch of his lips was light, almost teasing.

She wrapped her arms around his neck drawing Peter closer, trying to deepen the kiss.

"Oh no you don't," he warned, stepping back and wagging his finger back and forth. "No distracting me tonight." He ran his fingers lightly down her arm and gripped her hand in his. "Tonight is all about you." She noticed that he was trying to get a look at her apartment and wondered what he thought of her decor.

From the doorway, you could just see the tidy countertops of her small kitchen. Three steps from the door took you into the living room. Her space was small and neat. There was a glide rocker in the corner an oversized cream leather couch, with its back to the doorway, nearly filling the small room. A tiny television sat on a stand in the corner opposite the rocker. A coffee table comprised the rest of the furnishings and sat between the couch and the floor to ceiling windows. The window faced east and would have a great view of the rising sun as it peeked over the park across the street.

Curved brass and glass pole lamps stood sentinel over the couch and chair, providing ample lighting for reading. Tessa liked to read, and almost blushed at the number of books littered around every surface. A brightly colored afghan was draped over the rocker, and a matching one was folded neatly on the end of the couch.

"I like your place," he complimented her. "That couch makes me just want to snuggle up. Come sit with me." He kicked off his shoes and tugged her gently by the hand, leading her to the couch and encouraging her to sit. He placed two large, reusable shopping bags on the table and sat beside her, slipping his arm across the back of the couch behind her.

"Thanks," she replied, not sure if she was pleased he was sitting with her, or thanking him for the compliment to her home. They sat for a moment, just looking at each other and smiling.

"I gather you like to read," he said, with a wave toward the piles of books.

"Guilty. I read every day, and I read every night in bed. I'll read just about anything."

"I see that," he replied, taking in the variety of titles. Romances nestled with mysteries, sci-fi and biographies. "Have you read all of them?" There had to be thirty books piled around.

"Most of those," she waved to a pile in the corner. "But those," she pointed to the ones beside the rocker, "are part of my to-be-read pile. And don't even ask how many are on my e-reader or on the shelves in my bedroom."

"Wow. I read, but not like that. I'm partial to mysteries and military history." His fingers toyed with a wet curl of her hair. "I like your hair like this. It's kind of flirty, or something." He laughed at his own inability to find the right word.

Tessa leaned her head against his shoulder. The touch of her hair reminded her that it was still damp and she straightened up. "Oh, sorry. I don't want to get you wet."

He pushed her head back down onto his shoulder. "I'm fine. I like having you beside me. Even if I will come down with pneumonia later," he teased. "I took the liberty of ordering pizza. It should be here soon."

On cue, Tessa's stomach growled and they laughed together. "Good, I'm starving." She looked up at him. "Can I get you a drink?"

"You sit." He eased away from her and stood up. "I brought some wine. If that's okay with you?" He smiled when she nodded her agreement. "Just direct me to the corkscrew and some glasses and I'll serve."

She gave him directions and settled into the corner of the couch with her feet pulled up under her. "I could get used to this being pampered," she declared, raising her voice just enough that he could hear her in the kitchen.

"I could get used to pampering you, and you must be tired after a twelve-hour shift." He returned from the kitchen with the open wine and two glasses. He settled close beside her and poured them each a glass. After handing her a glass he draped his arm around her shoulder and eased her close. "Everyone needs a little TLC."

Tessa leaned against him. "The twelves aren't bad, you get used to them. I like having days off during the week." She sipped the wine. "Oh, this is good. Zinfandel?"

"It is. My sister had a bottle at my niece Jessie's birthday. I'm not sure you are supposed to drink at a first birthday party. But it was just family so we shared a couple of bottles." He laughed. "Avery, the birthday girl's mom, got completely loaded. Jessie had some troubles as an infant, and I worried sometimes how Avery was coping with having a sick daughter." He shook his head and rested it back against the couch, tipped it slightly until his head was just touching Tessa's.

"Oh, sick babies are difficult. What was wrong with her?"

"Nothing serious I guess. But she was colicky since birth. I've never seen a baby scream like that before. Poor thing was in agony all the time. Avery was so frustrated; she didn't know how to cope sometimes."

"What about her husband?" Tessa asked.

"Geoff is working overseas right now. Three weeks in, three weeks out. He took some time off, but they just don't have enough money for him to stay at home and help. Thank god, we have a large family. We all took turns visiting and helping out. The longest week of my life was when Av went for groceries."

They laughed together.

"She was only gone an hour, but it seemed like a week. I swear I don't know how she coped. But the weirdest thing is just a couple weeks ago Jessie stopped crying all the time. Now she's a normal healthy baby. It's like nothing was ever wrong. I'll tell you one thing though; my sister is a saint for having such patience. I don't know how she coped. I really don't."

"Colic is like that," Tessa commiserated. "I used to work peds and I saw some babies with colic that nothing could help. It was awful. You're right; it takes a strong person to cope. It's great that you found time to help out." Oh man, she thought. He's such a nice guy; pampering me, helping his sister out. Where had he been all her life?

"We rotated through. Av didn't want help at night; I guess it made her feel guilty. But she liked to escape during the day, so we took turns popping over so she could leave. At the birthday party, Av told us how much she appreciated our help. She got totally loaded and we had to put her to bed. I stayed the night to babysit." He chuckled lowly. "I really shouldn't laugh at her, but she was so damned funny. Thanking us all, hugging everyone and slurring on and on about how great we were. She was so happy." He chuckled. "What a treat to see her so upbeat again."

"Sometimes family is all we have helping us hold things together." Tessa smiled at the happiness in his voice. The door buzzer chimed and she stood up.

"Sit," Peter commanded, tugging her back onto the couch and stood up. "I've got this. I'm pampering you. Did you forget already?" He rounded the couch and answered the buzzer.

"You are bossy tonight." She laughed. "I'll get plates and napkins," Tessa offered.

"No need. I told you, I've got this. Plates, napkins, dinner, dessert, wine, the whole dam-darn thing."

Three minutes later he was dishing up pizza, salad and breadsticks onto the dishes he extracted from one of his shopping bags. "I hope you like supreme pizza, but if not, I got a cheese one too. We have three dressing choices." He waved the dressing packages under her nose. "I brought napkins too." He smiled smugly.

"Wow. I am impressed," she praised when he handed her a pretty floral, cloth napkin. "Oh, cloth too."

"For you," he replied. "A set of six. A little gift to thank you for having me here tonight." He offered her a loaded plate and settled himself on the opposite end of the couch.

Why was he sitting way over there when he had cuddled right up to her when he first arrived? Abandonment nagged at her. Defensively she pivoted on the couch, putting her back to the armrest and pulling her knees up in front of her to hold her plate. She felt her shoulders tense up. Had she said something she shouldn't have? Maybe now that they were here one-on-one without their friends to provide competition he was losing interest. Oh god, what if she was boring him? She gave herself a mental shake. Don't be silly, she warned herself. If he doesn't like you it's not the end of the world.

She hated when she felt like this, when the doubts Rick had created flooded her. Logically she knew that her ex had just been a nasty pig, but sometimes the insecurities he instilled in her tried to take over her mind. She took a couple of calming breaths and forced herself to take a bite of her salad.

Peter looked at Tessa as he leaned back against the other end of the couch. She looked tense. Her brow was furrowed and her shoulders tight. He wondered what had brought on the sudden tension. At Rob's welcome home party, Peter had noticed bit of insecurity in her and had wondered what happened to make her that way. Was it her ex? He didn't know the full story there, but knew that the bastard had hurt her. The insecurity he saw now was at odds with the confident sexual woman had has spent the evening with in the pub. He preferred that side of her and sensed that if he wanted to see more of confident, sexy Tessa, he would have to rebuild her strength.

He pivoted his legs up and slid one on either side of Tessa's legs. "This is nice. You can keep my feet warm and I can look at your pretty face while I eat." He wiggled his toes against her bum and winked. As he watched, her shoulders relaxed and her smile returned. Bingo! He had been right; she was worried that he was distancing himself. It was time to remove those doubts.

Watching her nibble on her salad, he contemplated the right tactic to take. He decided on a bit of flattery and caring. Too much flattery would make it seem like he had an agenda and too much tenderness might appear as if he was rushing her into his bed. Not that he didn't want her there he thought with a grin.

"You're grinning," she said, her fork stilling mid-air a piece of lettuce hanging precariously off the tines. "Do I have food on my face?" She dropped her fork on her plate and dabbed at her lips with a napkin.

He chuckled. "No, I was just thinking how much I like being here with you." Oops, too far he thought seeing her brow wrinkle.

"I mean, you are pleasant company, but your bum is really warm on my cold feet." He caressed her outer thigh with his left foot. "What do you think of the salad? I think the pumpkin seeds are a nice touch."

He almost laughed when she blinked owlishly at him. His abrupt change of topic must have left her off kilter. "When Otto told me he had a pumpkin seed, and orange vinaigrette dressing I thought he was out of his mind. Really, the guy owns a pizza joint. If I hadn't known him years ago I would never have trusted his impression."

Tessa took a cautious taste of her salad. "It is good. What is that cheese?"

"He orders it special, it's extra old cheddar." He waved his fork at her. "Go on, eat up. And don't give me any girly appetite, watching my figure BS either. I love your curves." He leered at her and winked again.

"Don't do that," she admonished.

"Leer?"

She blushed. "No, the winking thing."

"What's wrong with a wink now and then?" He winked one eye then the other before fluttering them both.

Tessa laughed. "It's ... disconcerting."

"Disconcerting? So, what's the opposite of that? Concerting?" He feigned a puzzled look. "Would you prefer drooling and leering?" He didn't wait for her answer. "Because when I look at you, I just want to wrap you in my arms and hold you close."

"Thanks," she flustered and looked away, turning her attention to her food, hoping to dispel the heat rushing through her.

Why does he do that? she wondered. The blatant flirting and teasing made her uncomfortable. She could talk to just about anybody, but his teasing set her on edge. Get a grip Tessa, she nagged herself silently. First you worry because you think he's backing off, now he's coming on too strong. Pick a direction.

"Oh my god, this pizza is amazing," she blurted with her first bite still in her mouth. She slapped a hand over her mouth in embarrassment and finished the mouthful. "Whoever made this is a genius. I've never tasted anything like this before."

Peter smiled. "That's Otto. The man can cook. I'll tell him you enjoyed it."

"To hell with that," Tessa said. "I want to marry the man who can cook like this." She smiled blissfully and ate another bite. Her eyes drifted shut as she chewed. She peeked open one eye when Peter laughed. "Don't you dare mock me," she warned, jabbing her fork at him.

He held up his hands in mock surrender. "Far be it from me to get in between a woman and her feed bag."

"Her feed bag," Tessa choked. "Oh, my brothers are going to like you." She narrowed her eyes at him, trying to look feral and dangerous.

"Excellent. I can't wait to meet them, because I'm going to be around for a very long time."

She felt light and happy. Pleasure warmed her heart and her cheeks. He wanted to meet her family? She did a mental happy dance. "I think they'll like you," she told him. "They like a quick wit and a bit of sarcasm. Just don't ever mention the parking lot. They can't face the idea that I have a sex life."

"Tessa, that night in the parking lot is one of my fondest memories. And I have no intention of sharing it with anyone. I'm holding it tight to my chest … and my heart."

In one smooth move he pivoted his legs to the floor, grabbed both plates and set them on the table. "Food be damned," he declared enigmatically and dropped to his knees on the floor in front of her. He braced one hand on the back of the couch and the other on the armrest behind her.

"I have to kiss you again," he whispered and swooped in to devour her mouth.

Tessa went still, her heart lodged in her throat. She swallowed once, then again. Her chest felt tight, like a band wrapped around it, squeezing just a little. His lips were warm and firm against hers, igniting a passion that burned deep inside her, stealing her breath. Her eyes drifted shut and she gave herself up to the sensations he was evoking in her.

Peter pulled her close, drawing her into the warmth of his embrace, his hands dancing along her back. She relaxed into him, enjoying the feel of his firm hands and moaning against him when his fingers tangled in her hair. With gentle pressure he guided her head, tipping it just right so he could deepen the kiss. His tongue danced across her lips, urging her to open to him.

It flashed though her mind that he knew just how to kiss her, how to turn her liquid and helpless to resist him. Then all thought was gone and her world was nothing but sensation.

The soft scent of citrus mingled with pizza and wine and tickled her nose. He tasted of tangy sauce, spicy salad dressing and of Peter himself. It was a heady combination that made her weak and pliable. She snuggled into him, but she couldn't get close enough. She moved her hands to hold him closer, her fingers buried in his hair as she pulled him closer. Her tongue met his, dancing and playing, advancing and retreating. Tasting. Their mouths fused, locked together and they savoured the taste of each other.

Slowly, Peter eased back and looked down at Tessa. Her eyes fluttered open and she whimpered a low complaint. He smiled softly and leaned in, dropping a light kiss on her nose. His hands stayed buried in her hair, lightly caressing her scalp.

"You do distract me," he murmured. "But I didn't come here to assault you." He kissed her ear and trailed his lips down her neck. His hands eased her head to the side, exposing her neck for easier access.

He kissed his was across the neckline of her shirt and up the other side to nibble on her ear.

His kisses were like fire, igniting her passion, making her weak with need, full of desire. Tessa moaned and leaned back, welcoming him. "Oh," she whispered, her back arching toward him.

He kissed his way to her mouth and gave her one final slow deep kiss. "Later, beautiful. You haven't finished your dinner. You'll need your strength." He gave her another knee weakening wink. "Dinner first, then, dessert. I brought chocolate." He smiled, handed her back her plate and settled close beside her.

She gave him a questioning glance. He was driving her crazy with his advance and retreat technique. She was crazy with desire for him. Her body thrummed and pulsed with wanting; but more important than that, her heart yearned for more. She wanted to get to know him better, to learn what made him tick and to be a part of his life. This game he was playing was wreaking havoc with her senses and with her heart, and she loved it.

She smiled at him. "Chocolate. You do know how to treat a girl."

Katie O'Connor

Chapter Twelve

"I cannot believe I am doing this," Tessa groused at Mitch good-naturedly. "I haven't golfed for years."

He tweaked her nose. "You'll love it. Think of it as a lovely walk in the park."

"Spoiled by a little white ball." She stuck her tongue out at him.

The day was beautiful. Last night's rain had disappeared under the morning sun and the world smelled fresh and clean. Tessa tipped her head back and let the sun bathe her face. She sighed blissfully and said, "Let's do this."

He laughed. "No pressure. Just tee-up and hit the ball. None of us are serious here." He waved toward two fellow officers who were joining them for the game. "These idiots can barely hit the ball. You can't possibly do worse than they will."

"Waters, you are such a liar," his friend teased back. "You are the worst fucking player in the group.

"Shh," he hissed. "I'm trying to woo her with my amazing athletic skills."

Tessa laughed. "How bad is he? Really?" she asked Mitch's friends.

"Brutal," Larry assured her.

"My eight-year-old son can out-golf him," Wil quipped before dropping his ball and quickly teeing off. He took two practise swings and whacked the ball on the third stroke. It flew straight up in the air, rising about fifty feet and dropped with a thump, twenty feet in front of them.

Tessa snorted, trying to hold back a laugh. "Wicked good shot," she teased and moved around him to tee up her own ball. Mitch handed her a club, she looked at it and asked, "Is this the one I want?"

"One wood. It should be perfect for this hole. Do you know how to line up?"

"More or less. Let me try, but if I mess up, I get a do-over."

"A Mulligan," Wil corrected.

"A who-again?" She shot him a glance.

"In golf, a do-over is called a Mulligan," Mitch explained.

"Okay then, if I suck at this, I get a Mulligan." She took a couple practise strokes, stepped forward and swung with all her might.

THWACK!

The club reverberated in her hand, sending shockwaves of pain radiating up her wrists to her elbows. Distracted, she forgot to watch where her ball went.

"Jesus."

"Fuck me."

Tessa pivoted to face the men, unsure of who had commented.

"What?"

"Sweetie, that must have gone 125 yards." Mitch snagged her in the arms and swung her around. "You beat the hell out of Wil."

"Woot!" she exclaimed in excitement. "Take that Wil. Maybe you want a Mulligan." She stuck her tongue out at him and winked. Laughter bubbled through her. She knew it was a fluke shot, but it was a great way to start the afternoon, even if her hands ached from the vibration and she wondered if her elbows would ever feel normal again.

"Why do my hands hurt?" she asked.

Mitch kissed her palms one after the other. "Your grip was probably too loose. It needs to be tighter, but not like you're trying to squeeze the shaft into a new shape." He massaged her palms gently, his touch soothing the ache.

"Oh, thank you, that feels much better." She ignored the off-color teasing coming from Wil and Larry.

Mitch and Larry quickly teed off, both with respectable shots and the foursome moved down the fairway, pulling their clubs behind them. Easy camaraderie prevailed between them and the three men included Tessa in their conversation and soon she was laughing and joking like one of the boys.

By the fifth hole, Tessa was only two strokes behind Larry, with Mitch and Wil another two strokes behind her.

"I can't f'ing believe how badly I'm playing," Mitch groused after a spectacularly bad shot.

"Quit trying to impress Tessa. She already knows you aren't a jock." Larry laughed.

"Why don't you take a Mulligan on that one?" Tessa suggested.

"No way," Mitch growled.

"Why not? No one here minds. Do we guys?" She looked back and forth between Larry and Wil.

"Not a bit," they agreed in union.

"No frigging way I'm taking a Mulligan." Mitch gave his friends a mock glare.

"What's the big deal?" Tessa asked beginning to sense there was more to his reluctance than just pride.

"Because if you take a Mulligan, the stroke is free but you have to buy the first round of drinks at the clubhouse. And since both of these jerks owe me a beer, I refuse to buy."

"Okay then," Tessa drawled and strolled down the fairway with an exaggerated swaying of her hips. She winked over her shoulder and added, "I don't mind beating you, Mr. Athlete."

Mitch roared and chased after her, laughing. He caught her quickly and she was fending off his tickling fingers when her cell phone went off. He released her quickly and told her to answer it.

She extracted the phone from her pocket and looked at the display. Her air whooshed out in a rush. Becky. It wasn't like Becky to call when she knew Tessa was busy. Foreboding crawled down Tessa's spine. Something must be up. A frown furrowed her brows.

"Hi Becky," Tessa greeted her friend. "What's up?"

She listened intently for a few minutes adding only mono-syllabic responses before saying, "Give me half an hour to get there. Hold tight. I'm on my way." As she talked, she returned her club to the bag and started rooting in the pocket for her wallet. She clicked off the phone and turned to Mitch.

"I have to go. What's the quickest way back to the club house? I'll catch a cab."

"Emergency?" he asked, concern in his voice.

"Not physical, no." She pivoted left and right, looking for a path back to the clubhouse parking lot.

"Who was that? Where are you going?" Mitch asked.

Tessa heard the confusion and irritation in his voice.

"Becky needs me. I have to go. Which way is fastest?" She looked around the fairway, undecided which way to go.

"She can't wait until we finish the game?"

"Sorry," Tessa said. "She's really upset. She wouldn't have interrupted the game otherwise."

"Catch you guys later," he said to his friends who had caught up with them. "Come on, I'll drive you," he added, putting his club back into his bag. "This way." He headed off down a small path to the left.

For a brief second, Tessa watching him walk away, his back straight and shoulders stiff. Surely, he wasn't angry that she wanted to go help her friend? Grabbing her club bag, she hurried to catch up to him.

"Hold on," she called at his retreating back. "I can't pull this thing that fast." He paused, his body tense and posture rigid, but didn't turn around. Tessa pulled alongside him. "Are you angry?" She stared at him waiting for a response.

"No," he snapped.

She tipped her head and looked at him questioningly.

"Yes," he amended and started walking.

"You're angry that I'm going to help Becky?" She shook her head in confusion.

"Yes."

"Give me a break," Tessa snapped. "You're mad because my friend needs me? Amazing."

Mitch stopped, and pivoted toward her. "No, I'm angry that my time with you is being interrupted." He puffed out a frustrated breath. "I understand that your friend needs you. It's just ..." he trailed off.

"Just what?" Tessa stared at him, hands on her hips, lips pursed.

"Look, I told you that I don't pull any punches. I'm angry ... no that's not it. I'm ... okay, I admit, I'm disappointed and maybe jealous." He pouted.

"Jealous? Of Becky?" She hopped forward and kissed him firmly on the mouth. "That's so sweet. Silly but sweet." She wrapped her arm around his waist and leaned into him. "Take me to Becky's and when I'm done, I'll call you and we can finish this date." Tipping her head up, she kissed his chin.

"Okay," he agreed grudgingly. "Come on, I'll drop you off at her place."

"You won't regret it, I promise." Without dropping her arm from his waist, she reached for her cart and moved slowly forward. "And, your friends won't be there," she added enticingly, bumping her hip against his.

"I'm holding you to that," he warned her as they climbed into the car.

Tessa laughed. "You'd better."

"Thanks so much for this," Tessa told Mitch, kissing him soundly on the mouth and unbuckling her seatbelt. "I know it's not fair to dump you, but she needs me. I don't know what's wrong, but Becky isn't the type to call for no reason." She rested her hand on his arm, silently pleading for understanding.

Mitch pivoted and stroked her hair gently. "It's okay, Tessa. I'm not that big of an asshole. I'm disappointed that our date is cut short, but I know your

166

friend needs you." He wrapped one curl around his finger and drew it to his mouth to kiss it. "Call me when you're done."

"It might be late, she's really upset." Tessa picked up her purse.

"Call me. I don't care how late it is. If it's too late for our date, I'll drive you home. Go now," he gave her a gentle push toward the car door. "Look after your friend. I'll be waiting."

Standing beside the car, Tessa gave him a grateful look through the open window. "Thanks Mitch, I appreciate this." She smiled at him. He was really a decent guy. She appreciated his honesty about being disappointed that their date was being cut short. But more than that she was tickled that after his initial reaction, he was being so genial about the whole thing, and unlike her ex, he was willing to share her with her friends, even on short notice. She could get used to an honest, generous man like Mitch.

"Go." He made a shooing motion and started rolling up the window.

Tessa watched him drive away. Yes, he was one of the good ones. Smiled and raced up the steps to Becky's door. The door opened as her foot hit the top step and she paused to blow a kiss to Mitch before stepping inside and closing the door.

"Becky, where are you?" Tessa called out.

"Bedroom." Her friend's voice was heavy with tears.

"What's up?" She kept her voice light, knowing that Becky would prefer it that way.

"I'm on suspension from work." Becky wailed. "They found out that I looked up Jake's phone number. I don't know how, but they found out."

"Oh, god." Tessa commiserated.

"Someone must have seen me flipping through the records. I have a hearing tomorrow."

"Did you call him?"

"What the hell does that matter?" Tears streamed down Becky's face.

"Will he vouch for you? Would he tell them he asked you to call him? It's rare, but if someone gives you permission to contact them outside work, it is okay to use the files to get their number."

"I haven't called him. I couldn't find the courage."

"Call him now. Explain it to him. Maybe he'll come to your defence."

"I doubt it. Fuck! Why did I have to risk my job over a man? I don't even like men." She paced restlessly around her bedroom.

"You really like him, don't you?" Tessa drew her friend into a comforting embrace.

"I do. I don't know why. All we did was argue, then have sex in the chapel. I still can't believe we did that." She shook her head. "But something about him …" She trailed off.

"Call him," Tessa advised, handing Becky the cordless phone off the dresser.

"I can't."

"Do it."

Reluctantly, Becky punched in the phone number from memory and Tessa slipped from the room.

Chapter Thirteen

"Hi." Rob kissed Tessa lightly on the cheek when she slid out of her car behind her apartment.

"Hi yourself." She smiled softly at him. "I'm ready to go."

"You changed already?" he asked taking in her walking sandals and shorts.

"I did." She pirouetted for him. "I had planned on going to the mall after work. I prefer not to stop on my way home because once I sit down after a twelve-hour shift, there is no way in hell that I am getting back up." She locked her purse and backpack in the trunk. "Let's go."

With unspoken agreement they headed toward Fish Creek Park only a few blocks away. It was their usual walking destination.

"How was your day?" Rob asked solicitously.

"Good. Busy. Tiring." She shook her head. "Sorry, I don't mean to be short. Becky had a hearing today, she contacted a patient's family for personal reasons. She could have lost her job. Thankfully, they let her go with a warning. The bastard wouldn't even answer her calls."

Tessa paused and stretched her arms over her head, trying to release the tension building in her shoulders.

"It was so hard to watch Becky suffer through it. Plus, I am exhausted from working extra shifts. My legs are stiff and my ass is numb from too much sitting." She laughed at herself.

"I hope it goes well for her," Rob comforted Tessa with his words and a quick shoulder rub.

"Thanks."

"II have the cure for that stiffness you know," he replied with a roguish grin and took her hand in his. His thumb caressed hers lightly as they walked along.

"Oh, and what would that be?"

"Tsk, tsk." He shook his head. "Patience, my dear. Patience. All in due time." He slung a small pack over his shoulder and offered Tessa his arm.

The evening breeze was nice after the heat of the day. Tension flowed from Tessa like air through a slowly leaking balloon. "This is nice. I needed to relax." She smiled gratefully at him and slipped her arm into the crook of his elbow. "I'm glad you insisted on this. I was stiffening up. I feel about a thousand years old."

Rob quirked one eyebrow at her. "Just a thousand?"

His arm slid around her shoulder and drew her close. Tessa relaxed against his solid warmth. "It's so good to have you home." She gave him a small bump with her hip. "I always miss you when you're gone. I wish you could be here all the time."

"I'm working on that."

Tessa stopped dead in her tracks and pivoted to face him. "Really? You mean that?" She shook her head. "I can't believe you're thinking about giving up the military."

"I didn't say that." He chucked her under the chin when her face fell. "I've put in for a liaison position at the base office here. There is no guarantee that I'll get it, but I have a lot of seniority from my time served."

"Wow." She threw her arms around his neck and kissed him soundly. "I'm so glad. I'm thrilled. I can't wait to have you here all the time." She punctuated each word with a kiss on his face.

Rob's hands cupped her checks and stilled Tessa's motions. Slowly, inch by inch he lowered his mouth toward hers. He paused, a hair's breadth away, and whispered, "I can't stand to be away from you. I need to be part of your life. Every day. I love you Tessa Dupree."

Warmth and happiness flooded her heart. Life was wonderful when you had someone to love. She poured every bit of the love she was feeling into kissing him, hoping that he could read her love in her response. The words 'I love you' didn't come easy for her, at least not to a man. To her family and friends, it did, but after all her disasters with men, the words stuck in her throat. She wanted to say them, her heart begged her, but somehow, the words just wouldn't come out.

She slipped her arm around his waist and started walking again. She felt Rob's small sigh rather than heard it. He was disappointed, she could tell. But she couldn't, no she wouldn't force the words. She did love him, she hadn't realized until recently how much. But she had told her ex that she loved him and it hadn't stopped him from breaking her heart. She closed her eyes and reminded herself that Rob was nothing like Rick the Prick.

They made their way slowly along the loop, through the park. They exchanged greetings with other evening walkers and made way for people on bikes or with strollers. There were dog walkers galore and the picnic area was brimming with families barbecuing.

The smell of wood smoke, burnt hotdogs and marshmallows carried on the light breeze.

Rob steered her down a small gravel path away from the bikes and dogs. They settled side by side on a bench overlooking the creek. The cooling air caressed her cheek, raising tiny goose bumps. A whispery sigh escaped Tessa when Rob's arm draped across her shoulder.

She pivoted on the bench, setting her feet on the seat. Rob's warmth seeped through her back. She leaned her head against his shoulder and pulled his arm down so it draped over her chest. They sat there, fingers entwined, Tessa growing more and more relaxed by the minute. At last Rob spoke.

"I bought you something today," he whispered in her ear.

"Mm," she murmured sleepily. Then his words penetrated and she brightened. "You didn't have to do that," she admonished gently.

"I did," he corrected her and set his small battered pack on her lap. "Open it."

She looked back and forth between him and the bag. "What is it?" she asked, knowing he wouldn't answer.

"Don't get your hopes up. It isn't anything special." He shrugged. "I saw it and knew I wanted to get it for you."

She eased the zipper open and looked at him.

"Stop looking at me. Just open it already." He laughed when she stuck out her tongue.

She peeked into the bag, her eyes widening in shock. "What?" She laughed and extracted a bakery box.

"Dessert," he informed her regally, feigning offence at her laughter. "Orange-chocolate cappuccino cheesecake, to be precise."

She whirled around and kissed him. "That's so sweet. I love chocolate." She jumped to her feet. "Let's go home and eat it." She grabbed his hand and tried to tug him to his feet.

"Or, we could sit here and have it."

She blinked at him.

"There's a small thermos of decaf and two forks in there too." He patted the seat beside him. "I thought a picnic in the park might be a nice end to the evening."

She plopped down onto the bench, cross legged, facing him. Leaning forward she kissed him lightly on the mouth. "Robert Gallagher, you are a fabulous man. No wonder I love you so much." Her eyes widened in shock at her words and she slapped a hand over her mouth.

Rob clasped her hand and drew it to his mouth, kissing it softly on the palm. "I love you too, Tessa." He smiled softly and kissed her wrist. "Now let's eat this and then I'll take you home and show you just how much I love you."

Katie O'Connor

Chapter Fourteen

Tessa puttered around her small apartment kitchen. Today was the first day of her days off. She had four glorious days before she had to return to work and she intended to enjoy each and every one of them.

She inhaled deeply, enjoying the tangy scent of tomato sauce, oregano and garlic. The lasagna was almost finished. She peeked into the oven and then turned it down. She didn't want it to burn before the guys arrived. She hadn't cooked a meal for someone else in ages. She was no slouch in the kitchen, but somehow this meal felt like a test. And not just of her cooking.

She had seen Peter, Rob and Mitch separately a number of times. But they hadn't spent much time as a group since the welcome home barbecue for Rob. Individually, they were a dream, but lately, she had noticed a tension when she was with one of them and the others were mentioned. Rob had hinted that the men had argued over her more than once. Peter and Mitch had confirmed her suspicions.

Tension crawled up her spine and she shook her head and twisted her shoulders restlessly. She didn't like the feeling she got when she tried to figure out where this was headed. Guilt wracked her, she felt so mean, like she was stringing them all along, but she was damned if she could choose between them. She dropped her oven mitts on the counter and rummaged roughly through the junk drawer in search of a corkscrew. She slammed things onto the counter one after another. Where was the damned thing? And why did she buy wine with a cork anyway? A twist top would have made more sense. Finally, she found it and swept the other items back into the drawer and jiggled it with just enough force to get the drawer shut.

In a couple of quick rough motions, she had the wine open, half a glass poured and downed. To hell with letting it breathe, she needed a drink now. Cradling the empty glass between her hands, she leaned back against the counter and took a couple of deep breaths. The warmth of the alcohol flowed slowly through her and she felt her hands relax their death-grip on the glass.

She could do this. She could spend an evening with all three of them. How hard could it be?

She heard them coming down the apartment hallway long before they pounded on her door. Their snappy words and harsh tones arrived before them. Great, just great, she thought. They weren't even inside and they were already fighting. For guys that were supposed to be best friends, they didn't seem to get along very well.

Every time she saw two of them together or worse yet all three of them, they fought over her like some kind of Neanderthals. It was driving her to distraction.

She sucked in a deep breath and tried to relax. It was no good. They were making her crazy and she had reached her limit.

She yanked the door open and glared at them. "I DO live in an apartment. I'm pretty sure the neighbors don't want to hear you fighting." She pivoted on her heel and returned to the kitchen, leaving them standing in the open doorway, gaping at her back.

Finally, Mitch nudged the others forward and they followed her inside.

Tessa stood with her back toward them, her shoulders stiff, her hands trembling as she poured herself another glass of wine. Peter reached over her shoulder and grasped her glass.

"Let me get that for you," he offered.

She yanked it back, the bottle in her other hand jerked and wine splashed out all over the counter. "I can do it." She filled her glass and drained it without stopping for a breath. "Sit. The lasagna is ready."

After giving her a couple of wary glances they filed wordlessly to the table and sat down.

Smack. A basket of garlic bread dropped in front of them.

Thunk. The lasagna dropped beside it, nearly flipping over. Mitch burned his fingers steadying it. He stuck them in his mouth but didn't say a word.

Wine glasses landed on the table with a clatter. Tessa carelessly slopped wine into them, heedless of the drops splashing onto the pristine white table cloth. The bottle hit the table with a thud. She slammed the fridge door after pulling the salad out.

She dropped into her chair without looking at them. "Eat."

"Tessa?" They spoke her name in unison.

"Don't," she warned them and started slapping salad onto their plates. Suddenly her shoulders slumped and she flopped back against her chair. "Sorry," she whispered, her voice laden with tears.

They made murmuring noises and patted her hands. She jerked her hands free and twisted them together.

"Do you want to talk about it?" Rob ventured bravely.

"No." She picked up her fork and tried to stab some lettuce. It scattered off her plate. "Dammit." She threw her fork onto the table in disgust.

"I can't do this anymore," she declared, lifting her head to glare around the room. "Did you think I didn't hear you arguing in the hallway?" She didn't wait for an answer.

Leaping to her feet, she paced the confines of the small kitchen. "You argue over me, you talk trash about each other. You push me to make a choice between you." She froze, hands on her hips, glaring at the dishes piled in the sink.

"Do you think this is easy for me? Do you think I want to love you all? Do you have any idea how fucking hard it is to choose?"

Their mouths gaped in unison, like a school of hungry fish.

Tears brimmed in her eyes and she blinked frantically refusing to let them fall. "Not a word," she warned them with an angry shake of her fist in their direction. "Not one fucking word, from any of you. You have nothing to say that interests me. I'm done. I'm just fucking done. Get the fuck out of my apartment and don't come back."

She stepped back and pointed imperiously toward the door. "Out! Don't call me. Don't text me, don't e-mail me. I don't want to see or hear from any of you again. Ever!"

Obediently, they stood and left the apartment. She slammed the door shut behind them and leaned against it, trying to draw a breath and contain the tears threatening to fall. They weren't worth her tears.

Through the door, she could hear them whispering, trying to make sense of what had happened.

She kicked the door with her heel. "Shut the fuck up and get out of this building," she screeched. "I'm not a prize to be won in one of your stupid macho games. I'm a woman and I deserve better than this."

Silence reigned and at length she heard them creep off down the hallway.

Defeat and fatigue wracked her body and she slumped against the door, sliding down to a melted heap on the floor. Three shuddering breaths wracked her body before she burst into tears.

Four days later and for the first time in her life, Tessa called in sick without actually being physically sick. She just didn't have the strength to cope any longer. She couldn't eat; she wasn't sleeping all she could do was sit and mope.

Every time she thought about her actions, she wanted to throw up. It wasn't like her to lose her cool like that. She snuggled deeper under her blankets and hugged herself. It felt like she had thrown away something special. She had really messed up this time.

She knew that she had waited too long, that she should have confronted them all sooner and told them how torn she was feeling and how much trouble she was having dealing with dating all three of them. Instead she had kept her feelings bottled up inside and let them play their macho games and revel in their Neanderthal stupidity. Sometimes she was such an idiot.

She yanked a tissue out of the box on the bed, blew her nose and pitched the used tissue in the general direction of the garbage can beside the bed. Empty tissue boxes and used tissues littered the bed and the floor and she didn't care.

"Life is so unfair," she wailed to herself. "Six months ago, I get dumped by the man I planned to marry. Then I have three great guys. Now I have none." She punched the mattress repeatedly, cursing with each blow.

"I should have picked one." Maniacal laughter escaped her. "Who are you trying to kid, Dupree? You couldn't choose and they wouldn't share."

She banged her head back against the wall, wincing slightly at the impact. She rolled it side to side, trying to ease the tension in her neck. Would they have been able to make it work if they had tried to be a unit? Would the four of them have made a life together? She knew other people who had made unusual family groupings work.

"Why didn't you suggest that?" she asked herself aloud.

"Because they are macho idiots and you know they wouldn't go for it," a voice came from the doorway.

"Becky," Tessa sobbed, stunned to see her friend in her apartment on a work day.

"I took the day off. Called in sick." Becky smiled at her. "I knew you were hurting."

"God, you can't take a chance like that now. Especially now. What about your suspension?"

"They let me off with a warning. I got lucky. Enough about me though. How are you holding up?"

"Mitch showed up last night. He looked like hell." Tessa sighed. "He was so haggard and exhausted, but he looked so good I wanted to eat him up. But I couldn't. I couldn't choose him and let the others go." She burst into fresh tears. "I sent him away." Her last word turned into a cry.

"What am I going to do?" Tessa cried, burying her face in her hands.

Becky drew Tessa into her arms and comforted her until she cried herself out. "What do you want to do?" she asked mildly.

"I don't know." Tessa hiccupped.

"Okay," Becky reasoned, "If you could have it any way you wanted it. How would that be?"

Tessa bit her lip and thought for a few minutes. "I want them all. It's so greedy and unbelievably vain, but I swear to God that I want them all in my life. Forever." She snorted. "Like that could ever happen."

"Would you really want that, if they were agreeable?" Becky asked cautiously.

"I would." Tears streaked down Tessa's face and she bit back another sob. "I can't help it. I love them all, enough that I can't break up their friendship. Does that make any sense?" She asked.

"In a twisted kind of way, it does. If you picked one, he would have to sever his ties with the other two or the tension would rip them apart anyway."

"I don't want to be responsible for that."

"Do you think they would go for it? For you being ALL together?"

"I doubt it. Their constant bickering and undermining is what messed me up," Tessa confessed.

"Truth now," Becky stood and looked down at her friend. "Do you want them all?"

"I do. God help me Becky. I want all three of them. I don't know if I can survive without them. I am in love with all of them."

"Okay then. We need a plan." She extracted her phone and punched in a text message. Seconds later her phone beeped repeatedly. She glanced at it. "Okay, the girls are on their way over. If anyone can devise a plan, it's the whole lot of us."

She gave Tessa a quick hug. "Now get your ass into the shower. I'll make coffee. We've got planning to do."

Several hours later they had eaten three large pizzas, devoured three pots of coffee and four bottles of wine, but they had a plan. It all hinged on Mitch's ability to talk sense into his friends. As a group, they agreed that since he had seen Tessa last and understood just how distraught she was that he would be the best candidate to pitch their idea to.

Acting on Tessa's behalf, Shayla had called Mitch and explained things. If they wanted Tessa in their lives, they would have to find a way to co-exist without fighting. Mitch had agreed to help his friends reach that conclusion. They had given him a deadline. Tessa's birthday was the following weekend. If he could get them to agree, he was to bring them to the party. If not, they were done for good.

Chapter Fifteen

Mitch slammed his empty beer bottle on the table and glared at Rob and Peter. His hands bunched into fists and he forced himself to relax. There was no way this was going to be an easy discussion. "Look, we have to discuss this. It's the reason why I invited you over." He glared from one friend to the other and met their return glares unflinchingly.

The past three weeks had been a roller-coaster ride for all of them. Emotions were up and down as they competed for Tessa's time and attention. Now they were holed up in Mitch's basement with a couple of beers under their belts and their testosterone running rampant.

Mitch stifled an angry sigh. Things had gotten so tense that over the past four days, Tessa had refused to see any of them, refused to take their calls, ignored their emails, and had shut off her cell phone to avoid their text messages. He had planned to stay calm and rational during this discussion. As a police officer, he knew how quickly these sorts of things could get out of hand. He also knew that they had to do something. They couldn't go on like this.

The playful competition for Tessa's affection had turned into a brutal, unforgiving fight for her love and it was tearing her apart. Sure, she had complained about it once or twice, to him and to the others, but it wasn't until he had seen her last night that it had really hit home. He had shown up unannounced at her apartment; she had threatened to call the police on him if he ever showed up again. Tears had streamed down her face when she opened the door to his persistent knocking. Her tank top had hung off her shoulder and she had lost weight. She had bags under her eyes from lack of sleep. But the most heartbreaking thing had been her broken pleading for him to just leave her alone.

What the hell were they going to do? That's what he wanted to know. He sure hoped he could talk the others into sharing.

"The two of you can just go fuck yourselves." Rob glared threateningly from one to the other. "I've known Tessa since we were kids. I've fucking waited for her to notice me for years. Back the fuck off, she's mine."

Peter laughed. "If she's yours, why was she climbing all over me the other night?" To his surprise, Mitch punched him in the stomach. "What the fuck?"

"I don't give a shit what you did with her," Mitch snarled. "Nobody talks about a lady that way." He high-fived Rob. "She's a beautiful girl and smoking hot and nothing you guys can say will stop me from continuing to date her."

"You fucking son of a bitch." Peter slammed a punch into Mitch's shoulder.

"I repeat," Rob declared, "Tessa is mine and I have no intention of sharing with either one of you fucking perverts any longer. I know how you guys go through women."

"You're not even going to be in town, soldier boy," Peter taunted. "Once you're back on duty, she'll have no one to run interference and keep me away."

"I'll keep you away," Mitch snarled launching his fist toward Peter's face.

Peter deflected the blow and dodged, accidentally slamming into Rob and knocking him sideways. Rob punched back, swinging wildly and landing a fist in Peter's eye and another one on Mitch's chin. Mitch countered with a kick to Rob's ribs and a knee in the general direction of Peter's groin. Then, all hell broke loose and the punches, kicks, knees, and elbows started flying. They fought like wild men for two or three minutes, only stopping when Rob's nose started bleeding all over the basement carpet.

"Fuck," Mitch shouted. "Don't bleed on my new rug; I'll never get the stains out." Looking down he realized that his own nose was dripping blood and that Peter had a couple of large scratches on his arm. "Jesus-cock-sucking-Christ. Look at us. Totally fucked up over a woman. Hang on and stop bleeding."

He disappeared into the bathroom and returned with a couple of wet cloths and towels. They tidied themselves up as best they could, all the while glaring at each other. Suddenly, Peter began to laugh.

"What the fuck is so funny, asshole?" Rob snarled.

"We are." It was all Peter could do to force the words out between fits of laughter.

"What the hell are you talking about?" Mitch demanded.

"Us. We've been friends for years. Not once have we ever argued over a woman. I would never have guessed we shared the same taste in women." He laughed again. "Now here we are beating the shit out of each other over Tessa."

"Point?!" Rob growled.

Mitch started laughing along with Peter. "He's got a point." He slapped Peter on the back and laughed some more. "Really, it doesn't matter a fucking bit what we want, Tessa is the one who'll decide. We can beat each other to death and it won't matter a whit." He broke off into gales of laughter and dropped to the floor.

Peter dropped into a chair and laughed right along with him.

"You guys are fucking nuts," Rob declared, fighting the urge to laugh himself. "Tessa is mine and I have no intention of sharing her."

"Man, you have no choice. Suck it up." Peter went serious for a moment. "Let Tessa decide. She's not a bone for a bunch of dogs to scrap over. She's a living, breathing, intelligent woman. She can make up her own mind."

Rob sat on the edge of the sofa, his elbows on his knees. "Fuck. Fuck. Pissy fuck." He punctuated each word by slamming his fist into his other palm. "I finally get her to admit she's interested in me as more than a friend and you bastards come along and fuck it up. Give a guy a fucking break."

They lapsed into silence and glared at each other. At length, their angry postures relaxed and the long-time bonds of friendship allowed them to be realistic. It really didn't matter how many blows they threw, or how many bruises they suffered; in the end it all came down to what Tessa wanted. Only she could decide who she wanted, if she wanted any of them.

"Okay," Mitch said after a long silence. "I have an idea." The other two men looked at him expectantly. "I can't live without Tessa. I love her and I can't give her up." Just the thought of living without Tessa made him sick to his stomach.

"Shut the fuck up," Peter growled menacingly.

"No, hear me out. The three of us have been friends for years. We've been through a lot together." Silently Mitch hoped that he could convince his friends that his hare-brained plan had merit.

"Point?" Rob snapped.

"I'm not prepared to give up Tessa, but I'm reluctant to give up our friendship either." He looked from friend to friend. "It kills me to say this, but …" he trailed off.

"But what?" Peter and Rob asked in unison.

"But I think I could share her with you guys. Long term." He held up a hand to forestall their arguments. "I've been thinking, really thinking. Look at Daniel, Douglas, and Tammy. They're making it work." Tammy and her twins weren't the only people he knew who were trying to make a go of a multi-partner marriage, but theirs was the strongest.

"They're twins, idiot." Rob said, shaking his head.

"True, but we're as close as brothers. Hell, I'm closer to you guys than I am with my own brother. I think we could make it work. Give it some thought. No spur of the moment, rash decisions." Mentally, he crossed his fingers, hoping they would see his side of this. Without an agreement, none of them could have Tessa. And that would be the burden that irrevocably shattered the friendship the three men shared.

They sat in silence for a while.

"But … never mind," said Peter with a shake of his head and Rob scowled at him.

"You bastards can just back off my girl," Rob threatened.

"You're missing the point, Rob," Mitch cajoled. "It's been weeks and Tessa can't choose

187

between us. Is it really even fair to ask her? I went over there the other night. She's a wreck. She's not eating, not sleeping. She's losing weight. She wouldn't even let me in. I'm worried sick about her."

"Fuck! Shit!" Peter and Rob declared in one voice.

"What do we do?" Their posturing subsided under their mutual concern.

Peter glared at his friends. "Don't make this more complicated than it already is. I think I've loved Tessa since I first set eyes on her in The Pub. Rob, I've known you loved her for ages, and I can hear it in your voice every time you talk about her. And you Mitch, I've never ever seen you so smitten. In all the years I've known you, you've never dated a woman more than twice." He slapped his hands down on the arms of his chair. "Don't you fuckers get this? I can't live without her and I don't think either of you can."

"He might be right," Mitch agreed. "I love Tessa. As a man it goes against almost everything I believe in to confess to a softer side. I hate to admit it out loud, but I do love her and can't imagine being without her." He shook his finger in Rob's face. "And you might as well admit it too."

"No way!" Rob stood and paced the room. Ten minutes later he smiled sheepishly and admitted his love. "Okay, hypothetically speaking, how do we share?"

"More importantly, how do we convince Tessa that it is okay to share?" Peter countered.

Mitch smiled. "Here's the plan …."

Chapter Sixteen

Tessa and Shayla stowed the beer cooler under the picnic table and unfolded the lawn chairs. They were the first to arrive at the campground and had quickly scoped out the prime camping spot and claimed it as their own. Now, the tent trailer was set up, the beds made and everything was ready to go.

"Done." Shayla decreed happily. "Beer time." Digging into the cooler, she extracted two cans and tossed one to her friend.

Tessa caught it, popped the top and chugged gratefully on the cool liquid. "I can't believe you managed to book the entire campground for the weekend." She fanned herself by flapping the neckline of her tank top.

"That is the advantage of having friends in high places." Shayla laughed and flopped into a lawn chair. He brother had created a private campground on the back edge of his property, close to the mountains. With its small man-made lake, playground and large treed stalls, it was a popular summer destination for a lot of people. "He's given us the entire campground for three days. He closed it to the public, so we can run free and party to celebrate your birthday. His only caveat is that everyone hands over their car keys, no drinking and driving."

"I can't say that's a bad idea. Who did you invite to this shindig?" Tessa asked, easing herself into a chair. She tipped her head back and closed her eyes, soaking up the sun peeking through the towering pine trees that surrounded their camping spot. She inhaled deeply, the scent of pine and fresh air rejuvenating her. "Damn, that smells good. Beats the hell out of smog."

"All the girls are coming," Shayla replied to the earlier question. "I guess Kelly and Megan are bringing their new guys. I can't wait to meet them." She snickered. "All three of your boy toys are coming, as are a few other friends."

"I can't believe you invited them," Tessa whined. "I don't think I'm up to facing them. Has Mitch said anything to you about the plan?"

"He hasn't said anything. But when he called and asked if they could come to your birthday weekend, I didn't have the heart to tell him no," Shayla said apologetically. "I think something good could come out of the weekend. Maybe a relationship or the end to it all. But a conclusion of some sort."

Tessa sighed. "I guess you're right. This needs to end one way or the other." She looked around the campsite, taking in the huge pine trees and listening to the chirping of birds and the chattering of squirrels. "Either way, I'm not going to let it mess up my weekend."

Tessa exhaled deeply. "I am so glad to be here." The last two weeks had been crazy. Working twelve-hour shifts was a mixed blessing. She had a lot of days off, with every second weekend being a three-day weekend, but twelve-hour shifts made for a long day. Still, that was what you got when you worked in health care. As a unit clerk at the hospital, her job was more mental than physical, but it was still tiring.

Add into that her royal blowout and breakdown, and she was exhausted. Dating three men at once had turned out to be a bit more trouble than she anticipated. Dating was bad enough, but Tessa had been trying to see all three men equally and that wasn't easy with their diverse schedules. Rob's leave was over, but he was still in town and working erratic shifts.

"I kind of wish it were just us girls," Tessa confessed after a long sip of her beer. "I don't know if I want to see them all again. What if they don't agree to the plan?"

"Come on, how could they pass you up?" Shayla laughed.

"That's exactly what I thought at first." Tessa sighed. "I'm greedy, I want them all. I want all the attention and I won't even get into the sex. Oh my god, all that fabulous sex all the time. I don't want to give that up. It's so selfish, but I can't help myself."

"Ya," Shayla quipped. "That sounds real rough. I'm not sure how you handled it." Then, in her usual blunt fashion, she added, "Why don't you just pick one and kick the other two to the curb?"

Tessa didn't answer immediately. She had lost track of the number of times she considered that option. Could she pick just one man? The question barely formed in her mind when she rejected it, again.

"How could I choose?" she whispered.

"Who do you love the most?" Shayla asked, unusually serious. They had been over all of this over and over again the other night.

Tessa knew her friend was just playing devil's advocate and helping Tessa be sure she knew what she was heading into.

"It's more than that," Tessa explained. After a long, slow sip of her beer she continued. "They all have a piece of my heart."

"Pick the cutest one. The hottest one? The one with the most money? Keep them all?" Shayla suggested with a smirk. "I know I would." She sobered and added, "There must be something that sets them apart, something that captures your heart."

Tessa glanced at Shayla and then closed her eyes and dropped her head back. She knew her friend was trying to make her consider her problem from all angles. "They're all such great guys. It doesn't matter who I am with, I am happy. When I'm with Peter, I think he's the one. Then Mitch calls and I think he might be. At least until I'm with Rob, then I think he's the perfect one."

"So, tell me about them." She gave Tessa an assessing stare. "Tell me what makes them special. No filters, no lies. Just give me your honest gut thoughts on each of them. Use me as your sounding board like we did in high school. Rob first."

"Rob." Tessa finished her beer and tossed the can into the recycling tub. "I've known Rob since grade six. We've been friends since he punched Freddy Schmidt for throwing dirt in my eyes. It was my first day at that school. Over the years we became best friends. I had no idea that he loved me until I gave him a ride home when he came back from this tour. When he kissed me at the airport, he poured all his love into it, and damned if I didn't think I might love him too."

"Wow."

"He's such a considerate lover, a giver and a taker. He makes me squirm and goes so, so slow. And all those muscles." She sighed. "He's kind and giving and treats me like a princess. He loves word games, just like I do."

"Oh my god, spare me from the word games." Shayla laughed. It was a long-standing mock-issue between them. Tessa loved word games, Shayla loved playing poker. "And the other two?" Shayla prompted.

"Peter, holy hell. I've never ever been fucked like I was that night in the parking lot. And he's got this thing he does. I don't know how to describe it. He's the master of the non-sexual touch. He can touch my wrist and I'm on high alert instantly. Or my hair, or my elbow. He leads in the bedroom, not in a bossy or controlling way, but as a lover. He likes to direct things, and he does it so well." Tessa squirmed in her chair. "Fuck, I'm getting horny just thinking about it. We can talk about anything. We love the same movies and books. Share the same philosophies. It is almost uncanny how well we get along."

"Nice. What about Mitch?" Standing, Shayla wandered over to the picnic table and returned with a bag of chips, popped it open and held the bag out. "Chip?"

Tessa ignored the gesture. "Mitch. Oh my god. He loves anal. Who would have thought I would like it?" Tessa groaned. "He is dominant in the bedroom. He can wring the smallest or largest response out of me without even trying. Geez, can you imagine me being submissive?"

"No fucking way. You don't have a submissive bone in your body," Shayla declared.

"Wrong. With Mitch, it feels right. I can't get enough of it. But with Rob and Peter, I don't need it. Does that make any sense at all?"

"Not a bit." Shayla paused. "Maybe it does. Go on."

"He's so good with his hands."

"Do tell," Shayla interrupted with an exaggerated wink.

"Not like that." Tessa laughed. "Okay like that. But I mean he sketches and does woodworking. You should see what he makes. We've spent hours together, with me knitting and him carving while we watch movies or listen to music. He's so comfortable to be around. He says he loves me." She sighed. "They all do." She stood up, arms wrapped around herself. Her voice dropped to a whisper. "And I think I love them all."

Shayla stood and took Tessa into her arms. "You do have problems, don't you?" she asked quietly. "Don't rush a decision. Take your time. Only a fool would make a rash decision involving their heart." She stepped back and grinned. "Besides, if they're all accepting the status quo of having to share, keep it that way. Oh my god, have you done them all together?"

"I wish." Tessa blurted and slapped a hand over her mouth. "Shit."

She was saved from a snappy retort from her friend by the arrival of a number of cars. It took a while to get everyone to their spots and get them set up. Shayla had come armed with a plan. All the families with small kids were parked near the playground. She had even arranged for a group of teenage girls to babysit for the weekend so the parents could have some freedom. Singles and couples without kids were parked closer to the bonfire area which was sure to become party central. That's where Mitch, Rob, and Peter were settled with their huge motor home.

The weekend was all about Tessa, and as everyone arrived, they greeted Tessa with hugs, kisses and small gifts. It was making her uncomfortable.

Mitch, Peter and Rob were vying for her attention, none of them willing to back off or give up and giving her no indication that they were willing to share her. The only plus was that they weren't fighting over her.

Finding Shayla, Tessa told her she was going for a walk and started off down the pathway of crushed red shale that circled the campground and wove in and out through the woods. Only minutes into her walk, the towering trees blocked the raucous sounds of the campers and she breathed a sigh of relief.

Katie O'Connor

Chapter Seventeen

Tessa slowed her pace, allowing the peace and tranquility of nature her to seep in and relax her as she walked along the path through the trees. Abruptly, the trees thinned to reveal a bench in a small, grassy clearing. It looked like the clearing had been created as a picnic area. Hidden under the trees were a number of picnic tables, benches, and Adirondack chairs. It was peaceful, but Tessa could easily picture the area full of families with a game of football going on in the middle. Grateful to get off her feet, she stretched out on a bench on her back to enjoy the sun and unwind. Sometime later, the sound of footsteps woke her.

"Here you are. I've been looking for you," Mitch commented when she sat up to look at him. He cupped the back of her head in his hand, leaned in and kissed her softly. "You look beautiful with the sun shining in your hair. It looks like it's touched with fire and gold." He sat beside her and draped his arm across her shoulder. "I've missed you." He kissed her cheek lightly.

"Hi Mitch." She leaned her head on his shoulder. There was no sense even trying to maintain her distance from him. Her body craved his, her heart longed to be with him. Allowing herself to enjoy his presence, she rested against him. He smelled of soap and man. His breath was soft on her face and held just a hint of chocolate. They sat together enjoying the sun and talking of trivialities for a few moments.

"We have to talk." Mitch looked her in the eye. "Are you sure this is what you want? You're important to me. I don't want to rush you, but I don't want to lose you either." Impatience creased his brow.

"It is what I want. And the decision wasn't easy," Tessa told him. The question did not surprise her; she knew it was coming, but still wasn't prepared to answer it.

"Mitch, I love you all. You're all important to me, as friends and lovers. I don't know how to explain it," she confessed. "Honestly, I can't choose. I don't want to. If I can't have you all I will just walk away." How could she settle on just one of the wonderful men that filled her heart and made her life so enjoyable? The very thought made her heart break, but how could she possibly cut two of them out of her life? Her decision was only made more difficult knowing that they were all friends, and no matter who she ended up with, she would be in constant contact with the others. Their friendship was making her life unbearable. It had gotten to the point where she wasn't sure if the benefits of dating them outweighed the negatives and stresses.

She gave him an assessing, pleading look. "I know it isn't fair to the three of you, but I have to be honest about what I need." She kissed his cheek.

Mitch sighed heavily and then gave her a small smile. "I guess I have no choice, do I? You're in control, and frankly I'm not used to having someone else in charge of my life, and my heart." He tangled his fingers in her hair. "But I am going to give you something to think about." He took her into his arms.

Tessa looked up at Mitch, her heart aching. How could love hurt like this? How could it be so perfect and so difficult? How could she have fallen in love with three men all at once?

"I love you Tessa Dupree," he declared, tipping his head to the left and studying her for a long moment before leaning in and kissing her.

Longing rushed through her at the touch of his lips. She pressed tight against him, returning the gentle pressure of his kiss and increasing it. Fire exploded through her at the touch of his lips. She kissed him back, hard and aggressive, her actions conveying all the pent-up emotions and feelings she was not able to express in words. Cupping his face between her hands she kissed him long and deep. Mitch's hand dropped to Tessa's side, stroking her waist his fingertips gliding softly against her sensitive skin.

His fingers wiggled their way under her knit tank top and Tessa's breath caught at the feel of their rough pads against her soft skin. Sliding off the bench, to kneel beside her, Mitch pushed Tessa back until she was once again lying on the bench. She rolled toward him, but he pushed her back with a gentle touch.

"Don't move," he whispered. "Just lay back and enjoy. Don't think, just feel."

After several weeks of dating, Tessa was accustomed to Mitch's need to be in charge of their love-making. She enjoyed letting him take control, but this was different. There was no command in his voice; his words were tender and almost pleading. She peeked at him with one eye.

"Keep your eyes closed, stop thinking. Stop analyzing everything. Shut your busy little mind off." He massaged her arm with long relaxing strokes, whispering endearments. Tessa felt the tension his arrival had re-kindled flow out of her and sighed deeply. Mitch had always had a knack for knowing just what she needed, even when her own mind and body didn't know.

"Let your body, and your soul take charge. Let your heart lead you," he advised, and slowly, his touch turned from relaxing to enticing, then to decidedly erotic. He teased her arm, her shoulder, and her abdomen. His lips followed the path his hands had taken and Tessa gave herself up to the seduction. She wanted this, needed this. She craved what this man offered, and was willing to take it all.

His mouth found her breasts through her top and she arched against him. Her nipples pebbled and hardened. Her breathing accelerated. Cool air caressed her stomach as he flipped the button on her black denim shorts free and eased the zipper down. Mitch's hand slipped inside her shorts and panties to caress her belly and she arched against him. She wiggled against his hand, his teasing and playing fueling Tessa's desire. With each wiggle, her shorts slipped lower.

"Lift your hips, Tessa," Mitch whispered and she obeyed without thinking. "Shift down." He moved to the end of the bench and urged her to come closer. His fingers delved lower, finding her damp core. "Oh my, you're wet already. Aren't you the eager beaver this afternoon?" he teased.

Tessa flushed with embarrassment, but didn't respond to his teasing. His thumb traced small circles over her clit. Around and around he caressed, teasing, quickly bringing her to the brink then backing off. Her knees fell apart, granting him better access, silently pleading with him for more.

Mitch eased her legs onto his shoulders. Kneeling and bending low, he placed long slow kisses on her belly and smooth mound. "Remind me to thank the man who discovered laser hair removal," he quipped lightly and trailed lower, licking and tasting. Desire swamped her.

Tessa whimpered and arched against his mouth. Mitch murmured wordless encouragement, his tongue flicking lightly over her clit, and slid one finger inside her. Tessa gripped his head, pulling Mitch closer and urging him on. She bucked against him and he pulled his finger free.

"Don't stop," she cried in dismay. Mitch slid two fingers inside her, pumping slowly, his fingers matching his tongue, stroke for stroke. His other hand reached up to caress her breast. He tweaked her nipple and rolled it between his thumb and index finger, pulling gently, just the way she loved it.

Mitch tugged on her nipple with one hand, sliding his fingers of his other hand out of her hot pussy as he pulled. He eased his fingers back in, releasing the pull on her nipple. He pulled and released her nipple, each pull in opposition to the motion of his hand. All the while, his tongue lapped faster and faster, driving her closer to orgasm. Tessa gasped and writhed under the myriad of sensations Mitch's actions were bringing out of her. His touch was gentle and demanding all at once and her senses threatened to overload her.

"That's it. Come for me, Sweetie. Give it to me, love." Mitch's words egged her on, tipping Tessa over the edge.

Tessa's pussy clenched and gushed. Her nipples pebbled harder and she gasped and cried out. "Mitch. Oh. Yes." Lightening exploded behind her eyes as she burst over the crest. Tessa groaned, writhed and moaned and at last fell still, her breathing harsh and uneven.

"Oh my god, that was fabulous." She gasped when she regained enough breath to speak. She looked down at Mitch where he kneeled between her legs. "Come here." She smiled. "Let me repay the favor." She tugged on his hand, pulling him toward her and easing herself into a sitting position.

"Not this time, Sweetie. This is all about you." He kissed her gently on the mouth and helped her straighten her clothes.

"I don't think so," she corrected, reaching for the erection tenting his denim shorts. "I need this too."

Mitch jerked to his feet and backed away. "I need it too. More than you can imagine." He grinned down at her. "But not now. Now, this is about you. My needs will wait." He rubbed his palm across his distended groin. "It might kill me, but I will wait." He tugged Tessa to her feet and wrapped her in his arms. "I needed to give you that, without taking anything."

His embrace was soft and loving; his hands traced the line of her back and came to rest on her hips. "Go, finish your walk. I'll see you back at the campsite." He turned her gently toward the path and patted her backside.

Obediently, she started walking. Tessa turned to look at him as she walked away. She walked backwards for a few hesitant steps, enjoying his smile.

"Go." He made a shooing motion with his hands. "See you soon. Get some thinking done, and don't forget that I love you."

With slow deliberate steps, Tessa continued on her way. Why hadn't Mitch let her pleasure him in return for the pleasure he had given her? His loving had been so different from their usual play. It was so gentle, so giving. Oh, her demanding lover was still there, but something had changed. And what about his repeated declarations of love? They were only going to make it harder when it all fell apart. She did love him, but she also loved Peter and Rob.

Tessa sighed and kicked a pinecone along the pathway as she walked.

"What the hell do I do now?" she asked a scolding squirrel in the trees above her. "When did my life get so damn complicated?" The squirrel continued to chitter away at her as she passed, his nattering tone seeming to tell her to make a decision, before someone, particularly herself, got hurt.

Katie O'Connor

Chapter Eighteen

Tessa's steps grew slower and slower and she rounded the loop back to the campsite. She was reluctant to return to the revelry of her birthday weekend. There was too much on her mind, too much at stake to rush a decision, and making a decision with all those people around was going to be impossible. Deep inside, she knew the time had come to choose. It was unfair to everyone to continue dating all three men. She had to get them to agree to a communal relationship, or walk away from all of them.

She settled herself on a fallen log just off the path. "Think dammit. Think. Think. Think." She chanted to herself. "Make a damn decision." She muttered aloud, verbally cataloguing the pros and cons of each man, hoping that hearing them aloud would facilitate her decision-making process. No such luck.

"Are you talking to yourself?" Rob's voice startled her out of her thoughts.

"What the hell are you doing here?" she snapped. "Sorry. I've got a lot on my mind. I came out here to think." She was instantly contrite.

Rob laughed. "No problem, Kiddo. Shayla mentioned that you had disappeared. I just wanted to make sure you were okay." He settled himself on the log, his thigh just brushing hers, his shoulder nudging against her.

"I'm okay." She paused. "I think. I've just got a lot on my mind today." She tipped her head and rested it on his shoulder.

"This is a party. You do realize that there is no deep thinking at a party?" he teased, pivoting on the log so that his legs straddled her hips. Rob pulled her tight against him, her cheek resting on his chest and wrapped his arms around Tessa's waist. "Want to talk about it?"

Tessa gave herself up to the comfort of his arms. "No." She sighed.

"Come on, I'm your best friend," he urged, resting his cheek on the top of her head.

"You're part of the problem."

"Oh." After a moment he added, "I suppose I should have known that." His hands stroked rhythmically up and down her arms. "Do you want me to leave?"

"Yes. No. Hell if I know." She growled low in her throat. "I don't even know if I'm coming or going," she pouted. "Stay a minute, I guess." They sat in silence for a few minutes, Rob's hands continuing their rhythmic, hypnotic massage.

"You really screwed me up you know," she told him, tipping her face up to look at him. "You were my friend, my sounding board. For years I've come to you with all my problems, and now when I need you the most, you aren't available. What do I do now?"

"Look at me." He tipped her head up so that she could see him clearly. "I can't help you through this one. I know that." He kissed her softly on the mouth. "But know this; I love you too much to hold you back. Do what is best for you. I've been in love with you for ten years. I've loved you since you punched me in the eye for picking on Becky Markham for being such a geek. One punch and I was a goner." He laughed.

"Oh my god, I had forgotten all about that. You were such a prick that day." Tessa shifted on the log so that her legs were draped over Rob's, and she was almost in his lap. She wrapped her arms around his neck. "Why would that make you fall in love with me?"

"You taught me something that day. I learned that I was a teenage jerk and didn't much like myself. You woke me up and set me straight. I waited years for you to discover that I was waiting for you." He sighed deeply and rested his forehead against Tessa's. "Now you discover me, and I've got competition from my two best friends. Sometimes, life just sucks."

Tessa smacked him lightly on the shoulder. "You're telling me that life sucks? You should see this from my side." Then she sobered. "I guess I've been rough on you. Why didn't you tell me that you loved me sooner?"

"No pressure," he declared. "I didn't want to pressure you. You needed to find me on your own." He shrugged and cupped her face between his hands. "And you need to solve this dilemma on your own."

Tessa looked up at Rob, searching his face for clues, reading his passion and love in his eyes. He did love her, she knew that. She also knew that she loved him and had for far longer than she realized. The other men she had dated over the years had never measured up to some invisible standard. Now she knew that Rob had been that standard all along. It was funny that she finally discovered her unknown standard at the same time that two other men met that standard. This was so totally screwed up. Her brows pinched together in confusion as she stared into his eyes.

"I don't like that look," Rob teased. "You need to relax, stop thinking so much and let your heart guide you." He tipped his head to the left, and moving slowly, allowing her time to pull away, leaned in to kiss her.

His lips brushed across Tessa's in a feather-light caress, then returned with a touch more pressure. She leaned in to him, increasing the contact, revelling in the warmth and love he was giving. She inhaled deeply. He smelled of citrus, mint and man. Was there a better smell anywhere? She snaked her tongue to taste his lips and sighed in bliss when she discovered that he tasted better than he smelled. Sweet heaven.

Rob kept Tessa's face gently cupped in his hands and deepened the kiss, taking her tongue into his mouth. Their tongues danced together as the kiss deepened. Tessa's hands slipped around Rob's waist to pull him closer, to caress his back and shoulders. His muscles were firm under her fingertips as they twitched and undulated at her touch. She loved the way his body responded to her caress. Power flooded through her, arousing her, making her need more. Her motions grew frantic as she pulled his shirt free of his shorts and worked her hands up along the bare skin of his waist and back. Rob groaned against her and trailed his lips across her cheek and down her neckline.

Tessa inhaled sharply at the fire his caress left behind and tipped her head further to the side to grant him better access. His hands slipped from her face and trailed across her shoulders and down to cup her breasts.

His thumbs stroked over her nipples and they beaded at his touch, hardening more with each soft caress. Her body came to life, she felt hot and shivery all at once. Her breathing accelerated until it came in short gasps. She felt electrified and alive, cherished and loved. Her mind was racing, valiantly trying to process everything she was feeling and trying to catalogue each sensation, to fix them in her mind. But it was no use. Her body was in control; it had taken the lead over her mind and she was lost to all but the sensations their caressing was invoking.

Rob pulled the scoop neck of her tank top down under her breasts and flicked the front clasp of her bra open. A quick motion of his thumbs and the bra slipped aside, out of his way. He sucked one breast, then the other, moving back and forth between them. Tasting. Pleasing. Loving. Tessa shivered under his loving assault.

She felt the snap of her shorts pop free and the felt Rob ease the zipper down so he could slide his hand inside. He caressed the flat plane of her belly and delved lower, to the moist folds of her pussy.

"Tessa, you're soaking already. What were you thinking of before I got here?" he teased, his thumb stroking back and forth over her clit. "It better've been me." He looked up at her and grinned.

Tessa ignored his comments, and writhed against his hand. "Oh," she moaned. "Please." Rob slipped one finger inside her moist core and pumped slowly.

"Does that feel good?" He twisted his finger back and forth as he slowly probed deeper.

Tessa bucked against him, her body so attuned to him that his simple caress drove her wild. He knew what her body craved and gave it to her with no teasing or delay. Rob worshiped Tessa's breasts with his mouth, his adoration in tune with the devastatingly perfect motions of his finger as it slid in and out of her and his thumb as it stroked back and forth over her engorged clit.

Tingles started at her core and became a shock wave of arousal and completion, overloading her with pleasure. Tessa gave herself up to the sensations and exploded in Rob's arms. Her orgasm was intense and unexpectedly fast: but it was delightful. She sighed in bliss, her satisfaction complete, and leaned against him.

Soft hands straightened her top and he kissed the top of her head.

"Um. Wow," she whispered. "That was fast." She laughed a bit. "And good. Very good." She buried her face in his chest, a bit disconcerted by her rapid arousal and peak. "Thanks, I needed that." She blushed beet red, thankful that his chest and her hair hid the color blooming on her face.

Tessa reached down to stroke him. His cock was rock hard behind his fly. He stopped her caress with a gentle touch. "Not now. Later. This was for you."

No pleasure for him either? Tessa wondered. First Mitch, then Rob, … it had all the makings of a conspiracy. She shook her head at her own silliness. Still, two men offering satisfaction and loving in one day, and neither of them willing to accept relief in return; it boggled the mind. It was almost beyond comprehension. Something weird was going on, and she wanted to know what it was.

"Why not?" she asked him, trying again to reach his zipper, growling when he eased her hand away.

"Just food for thought," he told her with a smile. "What are you doing out here all alone?" he asked in a blatant attempt to steer the conversation elsewhere.

"I went for a walk to clear my head," she told him. "But I'm not getting much thinking done." On the heels of that statement, all her problems came rushing back. She sighed and leaned away from him. She struggled to her feet and straightened her clothes. "Don't take this wrong," she said, looking down at him. "But I need to be alone for a while."

"Okay then." He rose from the log, "I'll head back. Don't be too long," he advised before adding, "I love you Tessa, enough that I'll give you up if I have to." He kissed her long and deep. "I was going to walk away weeks ago if you were still dating that knob, Rick. I think I will always love you."

Yeah, sure, she thought, watching him walk away. No pressure. Nope. None-at-all. Men were evil. Pivoting slowly on her heel, she marched off in the opposite direction to Rob. Hadn't Mitch talked to them? Hadn't he tried to convince them that the four of them could be happy together?

"Men are jackasses," she told the world in general. "All of them are evil, nasty and just plain rude. Do they think this is easy for me?" She turned a corner in the path and almost bumped into Peter.

"Well speak of the devil," she growled, steadying herself and backing away a step. "What are you doing here?"

"Camping?" he asked with a raised eyebrow and a laugh.

"Ha ha," she grumbled. "I meant here on this path?" She gave him the evil eye to prove she was serious.

"Walking," he quipped and then held up his hands in mock surrender. "Shayla sent me to find you. Supper is almost ready. And, since the party is in your honor, we thought you should be there."

Tessa studied Peter long and hard before taking him at his word. "Lead on McDuff." She waved in the direction he had come from. They walked in silence for a long while before curiosity got the better of Tessa. "Talk to Mitch lately?" she asked with a sidelong look at Peter.

"Nope. Is there a reason I should have?" He reached out and clasped her hand in his as they walked along. Peter pulled her tight to his side and wrapped his hand around her waist. She slid her arm around his waist and leaned into him. He was warm and strong, and being nestled under his arm was comforting.

They walked in silence, enjoying the sound of the breeze rustling the pine tops, the chattering of squirrels and the occasional birdsong.

"I could get used to relaxing like this," Tessa told him. "There is something so peaceful here. It's helping me unwind."

"Me too," Peter agreed. "I find peace in your arms," he stated as they entered the campsite. With that declaration, he dropped his hands and stepped away from her. He stood looking at her with a soft smile on his face. "You are one special lady. Now, let's eat." He gestured toward the heavily laden picnic tables.

Chapter Nineteen

The meal was delicious. There were barbecued hamburgers and hot dogs, potato, macaroni and green salads galore. There were seventeen different desserts, nine of them with chocolate, and a triple layer birthday cake. The snacks included chips, popcorn, candy, marshmallows for roasting, and all the makings for S'Mores. There was wine, beer, coolers, soda, juice, and water to drink.

After nearly bloating herself on the feast, Tessa settled in a chair by the fire to watch her friends in action. The men were laughing and joking about who was the best woodsman, and she wondered why everything became a competition when men were involved. Their primitive antics made her smile, and so did the fact that men and women separated into two distinct groups at these functions. The Gallery Girls were holding court with the other women present. The group laughed continually over several shared bottles of wine.

Rob's friends and neighbors had quickly fit in with Tessa's friends, and if Tessa wasn't mistaken, Becky and Rob's friend Jake had snuck off into the woods together. They had been arguing earlier and Tessa wondered if maybe they were going to kiss and make up. There had been tension between them from the moment Jake arrived and it had exploded gloriously into a shouting match about lies and deception. Becky and Jake had just met, but there were crazy sparks flying off them.

Thinking about sparks drew Tessa's mind back to the sparks flying between herself and the trio of men vying for her attention. She didn't feel right complaining about finding such a bounty of love, but if they couldn't agree to share her, she didn't know what she was going to do. She did know that she couldn't choose between them.

They were all such great guys. Granted, none of them were flawless. Peter was a bit of a workaholic and found it difficult to just veg-out and relax. Rob tended to be quiet and keep his feelings close to his chest; at least he had until the past few days. Mitch tended toward outspoken. At times he was almost too outspoken. Sometimes his blunt, no-nonsense attitude made her a little uncomfortable.

They were all kind and giving men. They loved dogs, cats and kids and if she could believe them, they all loved her as well. Like Tessa, they all wanted families and were close to their siblings and parents. Each man spoke to something inside of Tessa. Rob was such a gentle lover, sharing the lead. Mitch was demanding and aggressive and appealed to the submissive side of her that she hadn't even known she had. Peter was both giving and demanding in bed. They were all so different, and all so perfect.

How the hell could she live without any of them? How could she let any of them go?

Life was funny; for so long she went without love, dating weirdo's and creeps, and now she had too much love. Was it possible to have too much love? She had once read that the more love you give, the more love you can you have to give. Love wasn't limited, it was limitless. Every person you let into your heart made room for another. Was that why she was able to love all three men equally?

The raucous sounds of laughter drew Tessa's attention back to the women. Unable to resist, she stood and walked over to them. "Hey girls," she greeted them; sliding into the spot they made for her between Mia and Shayla. Tessa sipped on the glass of wine they handed her. "You all seem to be enjoying yourself." She smiled broadly at them all.

"Have you seen the beef here?" Shayla asked with her usual candor and gave a wolf whistle and waved toward a game of flag football. "Becky is ga-ga over Jake and I can't say I blame her." She waggled her eyebrows outrageously and everyone laughed.

Kelly smirked and gestured at Tammy. "And have you met her twins. Geez. It's not fair that one woman ties up two smoking hot men."

"Me?" Tammy cried with a laugh. "What about Tessa? She's hogging three of them. That's one for her, one for Shayla, and one for Megan. Or it would be if she wasn't keeping them all for herself."

Tessa forced herself to laugh with the others. She knew they were teasing her and that none of them envied her the difficulties she faced.

Mia turned to Tessa, the smile dropping from her face. "What are you going to do?" she asked seriously.

"I don't know," Tessa confessed. "I love them all and I don't think I can give any of them up." Then, to her immense mortification, she burst into tears.

"Oh honey, I didn't mean anything by that," Mia exclaimed in dismay. She hugged Tessa close and Shayla wrapped her arms around them both.

"It's not you," Tessa sniffed, accepting a tissue from Tammy and blowing her nose. She sighed heavily and looked from one friend to the other, further drawing all of them into her dilemma. "I love them all so much; they all feed a need in me. I feel so greedy, and so indecisive. But I've been stewing over this for weeks now and for the life of me I don't know what to do if they can't agree to share. What the fuck am I going to do?"

"Well, you've known Rob the longest," Mia offered.

"But I saw Peter first. Even if I didn't have his number," Tessa corrected. "I mean I know now that I've loved Rob for years, but that didn't stop me from falling for Peter and Mitch."

"Admittedly, they are all great guys," Tammy added her thoughts. "Do you really need to choose?"

"Can you just walk away?" Shayla asked.

"I wish I could," Tessa replied, "but this is killing me. And I don't think any of them like it much either." She swore and downed her wine in a single gulp. "Fill me up. I'm gonna get loaded. Fuck 'em all."

"Holy crap. I just got a visual of that," Megan laughed. "I think I need a cold shower now." She fanned her face dramatically. "Keep them all," she declared. "Tammy's got the right idea here. Why should you choose?"

Tammy interjected, "Hang on Megan; it's not all sunshine and roses. It takes serious effort to juggle two men, even if they are twins. Everyone has to be in agreement with the situation. I don't think my lifestyle is suitable for everyone." She looked thoughtful for a minute. "But it really does bear thinking about. But be careful Tessa. I love all four of you and I don't want to see any of you get hurt."

Tessa refilled her wine and took two big gulps. "Where are the rotten bastards anyway?" She asked the group in general.

"I saw them go into that monstrosity of a motorhome they rented for the weekend. They're all staying together." Tammy said. "It's crazy how much time they spend together. They're almost inseparable, and that is to your advantage, Tessa. As close as they all are, it could work. Maybe Mitch will be able to talk them into sharing. He seemed willing enough."

Tammy extracted herself from the picnic table and called to her kids. "Well, it's getting dark; it has to be near ten. I think it's time to put the brats to bed. I'll be back. Don't drink all the wine while I'm gone," she teased before she walked away.

Shayla and Mia stood in unison and gestured to the other girls. "Time for a potty break," Shayla quipped and in a matter of seconds, Tessa was alone at the table.

"Was it something I said?" she asked herself aloud.

"No," Mitch's voice came from the left. "I think they saw me coming. I scared them off with my manly scowl." He flexed his muscles for her and held out his hand. "Come see our trailer." His tone fell somewhere between a request and a command and she found herself obeying automatically.

The motorhome was huge. Tessa's first apartment had been smaller than this. It would have easily housed a family of eight or nine, let alone three bachelors. Two pop-out sides made it resemble a house as much as a trailer.

"Wow. This in nice. It is huge and so luxurious." Decorated in tans and blues it invited a person in to sit and relax. There was a small kitchen, a tiny but functional bathroom, complete with shower, and a living room area.

"It has two bedrooms too," Mitch informed her. "Peter sleeps in that one." He waved toward the back of the trailer. "Rob gets the foldout couch because he's the shortest and I get the master bedroom." He took Tessa by the hand and led her to his room.

"A queen-sized bed?" Tessa asked. "Impressive." She sat on the edge of the bed and looked up at Mitch, waiting. She had a feeling he had brought her here for a purpose and not just to show her the trailer.

"Lay back, test the bed. It's very comfortable."

Tessa slipped out of her jacket, kicked off her shoes and flopped back onto the bed. It was comfortable. She wiggled her way up the bed until she was dead center, her head resting on the pillows. She sighed in bliss as the mattress gave just a little under her weight. It was firm and soft all at once and felt like heaven. Sleep had been elusive lately with all the stress cluttering Tessa's mind. Work had been insane, but the real issue was the growing pressure to choose between the three men holding her heart captive. Tessa sighed again and yawned. She smiled sheepishly at Mitch.

"Sorry, I'm a bit bagged." It was an understatement, but there was no reason to let him know just how exhausted she was due to the conflicts of their twisted love lives.

"No worries, Sweetie. Relax." Mitch lay down on his side, propped up on one elbow and looked down at her. He stroked her face lightly, trailing his fingers along her eyebrows, down her nose, and traced the line of her lips. His touch was gentle, conveying his love for Tessa. She turned her head to look at him and smiled softly. Her heart warmed and she felt it might burst from the love she felt for him.

He massaged her temples with slow circular motions and a sigh of bliss escaped her. His touch was relaxing and hypnotic. "Oh, that's going to put me to sleep," she warned.

"You need to sleep. You look tired." He continued to massage her temples and hairline. Her eyes fluttered shut in spite of her attempts to keep them open. Although she fought against it, she couldn't stop herself from drifting off to sleep.

♥♥♥

A bright ray of sunshine intruded on Tessa's dream. She twisted her head, vainly trying to go back to sleep. She had been so comfortable, so relaxed. Sighing quietly, she admitted to herself that she wasn't going to fall back asleep anytime soon. She might as well get up. She rolled toward the side of the bed.

"What the hell?" she exclaimed. She couldn't move. Her hands and feet were trapped. She pivoted up as far as she could to examine her situation. Silk scarves tied her spread eagle to the bed.

"Ah, Sleeping Beauty awakes," Mitch mocked from the end of the bed.

Tessa turned her gaze to discover Mitch, Peter and Rob leaning against the wall at the end of the bed. "Let me up," she demanded with a glare. The trio huddled together, whispering quietly for a moment.

Occasionally one of them would glance at her and smile or wink. Clearly, they were up to something.

"I don't know," Mitch drawled. "You look pretty damn sexy tied up like that. Too bad about your clothes though."

That was when Tessa realized that she was naked. "Let me up now!" she screeched, writhing frantically on the bed. "At least give me a blanket," she pleaded.

"No blankets, no clothing, no freedom," Mitch informed her. "You shall remain our prisoner until we are finished with you." He twirled an imaginary moustache, and let out his best villain's laugh.

Tessa looked pleadingly at Rob and Peter. "Let me up guys and I'll dump him." She nodded toward Mitch.

"No deal," Mitch drawled and all three men smiled at her. Clearly Mitch was the spokesman for the group. He strolled over and sat beside her on the bed. With the back of his hand, he traced a line from her fingertips to her waist. Peter sat on the other side of the bed, mimicking Mitch's moves. Rob settled between her legs and softly stroked her inner thighs. The triple tease was light but sent shivers zinging through her.

"Let me up," she growled, trying not to give in to the sensations they invoked. "I want up." She groaned. "Now!" Her hips jerked involuntarily and she found herself twisting toward their light touches. "Let me up. Three on one isn't fair," she gasped.

"No dice." Mitch leaned in to kiss her belly button. "We have a plan for you."

Suddenly, hands and mouths were everywhere and Tessa forgot her objections to being their prisoner. They wouldn't really do this would they? Were they all going to make love to her at the same time? How could they? The logistics of it escaped her. But what woman hadn't thought of being the willing victim to two or three men at once? She certainly had. Tessa's cries for freedom turned to begging for more.

Two mouths devoured her breasts, honing in on her nipples while Rob teased her moist core with long slow strokes of his tongue. Three mouths and six hands, the sensations swamped her, bringing her body to life. Urging her on, teasing and playing, bringing her to the brink of orgasm and backing off. Suddenly she realized her legs were free. Wrapping her legs around Rob's head, she pulled him closer, grinding against his mouth. Her hands were freed for a second, and quickly tied together. She tugged on them, but couldn't free herself. Busy hands teased her and urged her onto her side facing Peter.

Peter drew her into his arms and kissed her deeply. Mitch spread her ass apart and something cold and wet dribbled against her puckered hole. She pushed back against the contact and his finger slid inside her. "That's my girl," he crooned in her ear, slowly working his finger deeper inside her tight nether opening. Two fingers replaced one, after a few strokes she felt the thick head of his cock nudging against her. Knowing her role, she fell still, pushing back slightly, allowing him access and in moments he was sheathed fully inside her.

Peter kissed her deeply and lifted her thigh to drape it over his hip. His long thick cock nudged at her pussy lips. Her eyes flew open and she stared into his eyes. "Sh," he whispered, and took her mouth in a deep kiss.

Mitch's mouth roamed over her shoulders and the back of her neck. He murmured soothing sounds in her ear and reached around Tessa to cup her breast. "Relax, babe, this will work if you relax."

Accustomed to following his orders, she forced herself to lay still and let Mitch direct her. Peter pushed his cock into her dripping pussy as Mitch pulled out slowly. Then they reversed. In and out they moved with slow precision. Tessa's pussy clenched and she felt herself, relax and open to their strokes. Quickly they worked out a rhythm between them. Tessa's eyelids fell shut and she gave in to the feelings. Peter shifted in front of her and she felt something velvety smooth and hard nudging at her face.

Her eyes fluttered open. Rob knelt in front of her, his cock poking at her face. Balanced on one knee, with one arm propped against the wall, he looked anything but comfortable. She raised her eyebrow at him and Rob grinned roguishly down at her and nudged her cheek with his cock. Twisting her head, she opened her mouth and greedily welcomed him inside. Her tongue darted across the head of Rob's cock, teasing and flicking. He groaned and bucked under her touch, but quickly settled into an easy pace of strokes. His cock glided in and out of her mouth in unison to Mitch's stokes in her ass. Peter worked in opposition, all three of them riding her, pleasuring her, their cocks buried inside her, their hands loving any part they could reach.

This was more than sex, Tessa thought. This was lovemaking. These three men were showing her their love, working together to please her. Her heart felt like it would explode, her happiness flowed over her and she burst into orgasm. Her pussy clenched, threatening to crush Mitch and Peter, but pushing them over the edge. Rob pulled free of her mouth and exploded onto Tessa's chest.

Someone freed her hands and they stayed there a moment, all four of them panting, trying to regain their breath and their equilibrium. Rob disappeared from the room and returned with a couple of damp towels. With loving touches, they wiped Tessa clean and settled in to cuddle her. Peter sat resting against the headboard with Tessa nestled between his legs, her back against his chest. Mitch and Rob settled on either side of them, taking Tessa's hands in theirs.

In spite of feeling wrapped in love, Tessa felt uneasy and strangely disconcerted. Their loving was full of ecstasy and caring, but they hadn't said anything about sharing her. Her body was sated, her heart full, but her mind was in turmoil.

It was a while before anyone spoke. "Um. What's going on?" Tessa asked quietly.

"We were showing you," Mitch said, kissing the top of her head, "that we are not asking you to choose. We spent most of last night fighting over you. We've even got some welts to prove it." He laughed and showed her a large bruise on his forearm. "In the end, we agreed that none of us could live without you. We also decided that our friendship was strong enough to risk the rewards of sharing your heart."

She looked at all of them in turn. Their faces reflected their love and sincerity.

"It won't be easy, but if you'll have us, we're willing to play nice and share."

"I don't know," Tessa hedged. "I don't think it's that easy." Worry filled her voice. "What if it doesn't work?"

"We'll cross that bridge when we get there," Mitch murmured in her ear. "Tammy told us about a support group for multi-partner couples. That's how Tammy, Daniel, and Douglas finally worked things out. I guess our situation is unusual, but not as rare as I thought it was."

"There is hope for us," Rob added, "if we are all willing to work at it. I love you, Tessa."

Mitch stroked her hair softly and she glanced up at him. "I love you," he whispered when their eyes met.

"I love you too. I don't think I could live without you," Peter added.

Tessa's gaze flew back and forth between the three men, taking in their soft, worried smiles. Could it really work? Could her life have taken such a good turn? What would people think? Suddenly she realized that she didn't care. She loved all three of these men and wanted to share her life with them for as long as it lasted.

A lilting laugh escaped her. "I love you guys. What would I do without you?" Grinning cheekily, she pivoted to take a cock in each hand and one in her mouth. "Yum," she murmured around a mouthful of rapidly hardening cock.

Who Is Katie O'Connor?

I'm Katie O'Connor. No, that's not my real name, just in case you wondered! (Snicker.) I live in Calgary, Alberta, Canada. I am a wife, and the mother of two kids who have grown up and moved away, and two cats who still live at home. I believe in dragons, fairies, UFOs, ghosts, and house pixies (and a lot of other silly things.)

I like to think of myself as a decent parent, a good wife and a steadfast and true friend. But you don't really want to hear how great I think I am. So, I'll stick to the facts (as I see them.)

I have dabbled in writing since my university days. There is some part of me that drives me to create stories and write them down. It is impossible for me NOT to write. I think my head would explode if I kept all those ideas trapped inside. I even dream story lines. I have thought about keeping a notebook beside my bed so I can start writing those dream ideas down. But then again, maybe not, because some of those dreams seem like fabulous stories while I am dreaming, but are a little suspect on closer examination under daylight.

My mind is a very busy place and the ideas just keep on coming. I have to jot them down some place, so my laptop is full of partially completed stories and dozens of idea files. For me, the most difficult part of the writing process is choosing names. Recently I went through some old files looking for a particular story. I had ten heroines with the same first name, so much for being creative. Okay, maybe I need a baby name book.

I've tried my hand at writing poetry, science fiction, adventures and romance novels. But my passion is, and always has been erotica. I just had to dig deep and give myself permission to write it. My parents know what I do, and I have told my mother that she will never-ever-ever read my erotica. Can you just imagine? I would die.

My husband tells me that I have a devious, sexual mind, and I have to admit that I like sex, a lot. (Shh, don't tell my kids, or my mother!) Or any of the crazy men my man plays lacrosse with.

Over the years, I have been a waitress, day-home mom, cashier, chambermaid, a lab and x-ray technician, and a quilting teacher. Currently I'm trying my hand at managing a small pet supply shop. It took a long time for me to discover my passion. I am a quilter by day and a writer of erotica by night. Having a secret identity as a writer of erotica is the most fun I've had all week.

Here's hoping you have enjoyed reading this and that it jazzes up your sex-life because we all deserve fabulous one! And no, I haven't done all the things in my stories. They're just food for fantasies, mine and yours.

Don't forget to check out my other stories available in all the usual places where digital books are sold. You can also find the occasional free read on my blog.

The Gift: Novella. Released 2011
Corralling the Cowboy: Short Story. Released 2012

I love to hear from me readers. You can find me …
Twitter: Katie O'Connor @KatieOhWrites
FaceBook: http://www.facebook.com/katieohwrites
Website: http://katieohwrites.com
Goodreads: as Katie O'Connor
http://www.amazon.com/author/katieoconnor

Hugs,
Katie